Cathie Dunsford is director of Dunsford Publishing Consultants which has brought 148 new authors into print in the Pacific. She has taught writing, literature and publishing at Auckland University since 1975 in the English Department and through Continuing Education, and was Fulbright Post-Doctoral Scholar at the University of California Berkeley 1983–6. She has co-directed three national writers' conferences, and her work has been published in the USA, Canada, the UK, Australia, New Zealand and in translation in Germany. Her writing has achieved wide acclaim and she is recipient of the Scholarship in Letters and the Established Writers Grant from CNZ Arts Council. She recently completed a book tour of Germany. Cath Dunsford believes readers are vital to the life of an author and welcomes your feedback: <dunsford@voyager.co.nz>.

SONG OF THE SELKIES

Cathie Dunsford

Spinifex Press Pty Ltd
504 Queensberry Street
North Melbourne, Vic. 3051
Australia
women@spinifexpress.com.au
http://www.spinifexpress.com.au

First published by Spinifex Press, 2001
Copyright © Cathie Dunsford, 2001
Copyright © on layout and design: Spinifex Press, 2001

Typeset in Sabon by Palmer Higgs Pty Ltd
Cover design by Deb Snibson

National Library of Australia
Cataloguing-in-Publication data:
Dunsford Cathie, 1953– .
    The song of the selkies.
    ISBN 1 876756 09 8
    I. Title.

    NZ823.2

Dedication

For Keri Hulme:
I hope this helps your Orcadian ancestors
to swim with your Kai Tahu ancestors.
We'll celebrate together in Orkney and Okarito! —
Nau te rourou, naku te rourou ka ora te manuwhiri.
(With your food basket and my food basket,
the guests will have enough.)

For Karin Meissenburg,
inspiration for Song of the Selkies:
Mahalo for your aroha, advice on the text and
your warm hospitality in Orkney.

Acknowledgements

The Broomsbury Writers and whanau: especially Beryl Fletcher and Susan Sayer.

Mark Weighton (artist), UK, for the stunning cover for this book. Mahalo.

Dorrie (author) and Donald (artist) Morrison, Stromness, Orkney, for their hospitality, local knowledge and great talks during the writing process.

George Mackay Brown (author), Orkney, for ongoing inspiration and for bringing the poetry of Orkney up from the soil and seas.

Tam (Stromness Books) for providing the best book-store in Orkney; and Gunnie Moberg for her exquisite photographs of Orkney.

Susan Hawthorne for sharp editing skills. Susan Hawthorne and Renate Klein for their vision with Spinifex Press, their wonderful support for the Cowrie series worldwide and their ability to get our work global and in translation.

Laurel Guymer for all of the above and her humour and energy while representing our books worldwide.

Barbara Burton for her astute copy-editing.

Maralann Damiano for her stunning production skills.

All the staff and agents of Spinifex Press worldwide for their dedication and support for multicultural literature. Jenny Nagle and the staff of Addenda for their promotional skills in Aotearoa. Karin Meissenburg and Global Dialogues for promotional skills at the Frankfurt Bookfair.

Doreen, Noel, Kevin and Debbie — for always being supportive through the process. Mahalo — thanks — to you all.

Cathie Dunsford,
Tawharanui, Aotearoa.

Preface

'In Keres theology the creation does not take place through copulation. In the beginning existed Thought Woman and her dormant sisters, and Thought Woman thinks creation and sings her two sisters into life. After they are vital she instructs them to sing over the items in her basket (medicine bundles) in such a way that those items have life. After that crucial task is accomplished, the creatures thus vitalised take on the power to regenerate themselves — that is, they can reproduce others of their kind. But they are not in and of themselves self-sufficient: they depend for their being on the medicine power of the three great Witch Creatrixes, Thought Woman, Uretsete, and Naotsete. The sisters are not related by virtue of having parents in common; that is, they are not alive because anyone bore them. Thought Woman turns up, so to speak, first as Creatrix and then as a personage who is acting out someone else's 'dream'. But there is no time when she did not exist. She has two bundles in her power, and these bundles contain Uretsete and Naotsete, who are not viewed as her daughters but as her sisters, as coequals who possess the medicine power to vitalize the creatures that will inhabit the earth. They have the power to create the firmament, the skies, the galaxies, and the sea, which they do through the use of ritual magic.'

Paula Gunn Allen, (Laguna Pueblo/Sioux Indian), *The Sacred Hoop, Recovering the Feminine in American Indian Traditions*, Beacon Press, Boston, USA, 1986, p.16.

'The mother of life. This is my interpretation of the rainbow snake . . . In the dreamtime, the rainbow serpent lived under the earth, everything lay sleeping, nothing lived. Nothing was dead either, but nothing moved, they were all asleep. Then the rainbow serpent broke through the crust of the earth and opened the way for all creatures. They came to the surface of the earth and lived.'

Kath Walker, Oodgeroo Noonuccal (Murri), Stradbroke Island, Australia, quoted in Ulli Beier, *Quandamooka: The Art of Kath Walker,* Robert Brown/Aboriginal Artists Agency, Sydney, Australia, 1985, p.24.

'They were nothing more than people, by themselves. Even paired, any pairing, they would have been nothing more than people by themselves. But all together, they have become the heart and muscles and mind of something perilous and new, something strange and growing and great. Together, all together, they are the instruments of change.'

Keri Hulme, (Kai Tahu Maori/ Orkney), Okarito, Aotearoa (NZ), from Keri Hulme, *The Bone People,* Spiral/Hodder and Stoughton, Auckland, NZ, 1983, p.4.

[1]

My story is from my Canadian Inuit grandmother and tells about the origin of the Sea Spirit. It begins when a young Inuit girl is forced by her father to marry a dog. After she has born several children, her father drowns the dog and her children seek revenge. They fail in their attempts and are banished. Then a stormy petrel swoops from the sky and takes the form of an ugly man whom the Inuit marries and she escapes with him in his kayak. Her father pursues them and grabs his daughter, so the bird creates a mighty storm to try to capsize their boat. The screaming father tries to throw the girl at the mercy of the bird, but she clings to the side of the boat. So the father begins to hack off her fingers at the joints until she slides under the water. This is how the sea people were created — the seals from her fingertips, the bearded seals from her middle joints and the walruses from the end joints. The Inuit girl drifts to the sea bed where she is transformed into the wondrous Sea Spirit, surrounded by the sea creatures created from her body. Her husband returns as a guardian sea dog and her father is swept out to sea in his sorrow, destined to remain an angry tormentor to those humans who transgress against humanity, a father who could sacrifice his daughter to save himself.

There are many versions of this story — but this is the one my grandmother told me. My uncle sang me a Netsilik Eskimo version where the tribe at Qingmertoq in the Sherman Inlet tie their sea kayaks together to make a giant raft and leave to find new hunting grounds. The raft is very crowded, so when the orphan girl, Nuliajuk tries to jump on board, they throw her into the sea. She grabs the edge of the raft and they slash her fingers off. As she drifts to the sea floor, the stumps of her fingers spring to life in the sea and rise to the surface crying like seals. And so seals were born into life. Nuliajuk becomes the Great Sea Spirit, mother of all sea creatures, and the most powerful and feared of all spirits because she controls the destiny of men. She nurtures all living creatures, including those on land — and is quick to punish any breach of taboo. She hides and protects her creatures when man does harm, and thus man starves, and has to call on shamans to help. She is a woman with great powers and we are taught to respect her. I will now act out both versions of the story without words and let the miming movements speak for me, speak for Nuliajuk.

The audience watches in silent wonder as Sasha becomes the raft, the people, the fingers, the wind over the water and ocean drift beneath the surface, the new seals and creatures emerging from the fingers of Nuliajuk. She plays a flute to mark the end of one story, the haunting sounds echoing up through the roof of the ruined abbey and out to sea, and then she becomes the girl forced by her father to marry a dog, taking on the shapes of the father, the dog, the stormy petrel, the kayak listing in the storm, the girl, as her father hacks off her fingers. There is a reverent silence at the end as the last of the story-tellers finishes and walks to the edge of the open-air theatre created by the walls of the ruined Tantallon Abbey high above the rugged Scottish Coast. Facing the ocean, Sasha plays her Selkie Song, dedicated to the Sea Spirit of Nuliajuk and all her sea creatures, on her delicately carved wooden flute, and as the haunting melodies float out over the hushed waters, Cowrie is sure she hears seals crying out in response.

4

[2]

'I never believed you could eat smoked salmon this delicious with steamed clams mounded like Everest and surrounded by Scottish sea creatures. Yum.' Cowrie is about to tuck into her meal when she glances at Sasha, then hesitates. 'Maybe we should offer karakia, a prayer, to Nuliajuk, and give thanks for this meal,' she suggests.

Sasha grins. 'Yes. We should.' The gathered story-tellers bow their heads as Sasha takes out her flute and plays. The crowds milling around the tables, swarming over Royal Mile, caught up in the frenzy and excitement of the Edinburgh Festival, stop a moment, listening to the haunting sounds of seal cries as they emerge from the flute under the skilful fingertips of Sasha.

Then the bustle continues, as the storytellers dig into their shared meal, excited and high after five days of hearing stories from around the globe, and inspired by the wonderfully diverse ways of communicating this ancient wisdom. Sun pours down on them from a brilliant Scottish sky, warming their bodies and highlighting the dazzling colours of the clowns and street performers and buskers. They compare notes on the virtues of performing at the Storytelling Venue on Royal Mile or at the open-air seaside abbey and both have different merits. But all agree that last night's performance by Sasha was a high point of the festival — and many others heard seal cries in response to the flutesong, though some of the locals doubt this.

Not far from their table, a mime artist plays a silent viola. He is waiting for something. The audience is not sure what it is. Suddenly he sees what he wants, and plays with feeling. Then he stops and focuses on another group. He stays silent until one of them smiles at him. He picks up his viola and plays. Gradually, people realise what motivates his play, and this brings a smile to their lips. Soon everyone around is smiling, even the tired workers from the Bank of Scotland who have to jostle the crowds to shop in their lunch breaks.

A circle of bystanders watches another street performer. He asks a frightened child if she could balance on his shoulders. The child nods no. She is afraid. Gradually, the acrobat teaches the child to have courage. First he stands the child on a box, then another box, then another, until she is at shoulder height. The young girl is encouraged by the cheers from the crowd. It is a small, delicate move to direct her from the top of the boxes onto the shoulders of the man. The girl hesitates. The crowd takes in a breath, recalling that moment of fear within us all, then the girl moves one foot, then the other, onto the man's shoulders and, guided by his hands, stands upright. Trumpets play and the crowd cheers as the girl gradually begins to smile, until her face is transformed by a wide grin. Now a small girl, who was terrified ten minutes ago, stands on top of the world, urged on by total strangers and her tentative parents who had never ventured this far in trust. The girl raises a hand to the sky, holding on with only one hand. She shouts in joy. Her balance wavers a few seconds, but she grabs the hand of the man and recaptures it.

The music celebrates her success and the crowd roars her on. Such a simple act, such a surprisingly simple act, that will stay in the memory of this girl forever . . . the day she bravely stood on the top of the world, before a huge crowd, on Royal Mile at the Edinburgh Festival. As she is returned to terra firma, there is a look of courage and determination in her eye that was lacking before, and her parents see their wee bairn freshly as they gather her in their arms, and smile at the crowd, awed that their daughter had such courage.

Up and down Royal Mile, artists and performers from all around the globe strut their stuff, keen to capture an audience for their night events or simply perform for the pure joy of it. The old cobblestones gleam from the polished feet of passers by and the exhaust-free street, cordoned off from traffic, becomes a human circus in a mass celebration of spirit for the weeks of the festival. Stands selling everything from brightly coloured jester's hats to paintings, hand-made books and clothes straddle the sidewalks and the atmosphere of celebration is infectious.

'You would not believe how amazing this is after one of the coldest winters on record.' Sahara sucks a clam from its shell as she tells them how cold and grey and miserable these streets can be in the dark of winter, how the snow and sleet make getting about nearly impossible and how delighted she is that all the hard work in organising the storytelling festival has paid off in the celebrations and atmosphere of the past five days.

Cowrie grins. 'Not as freezing as it was when we were in the Antarctic, Sah.' She winks. 'That should have prepared you for an Edinburgh winter.'

'Yes, but we expected the cold there and were prepared. I came here in the summer for my first festival so I was shocked when winter came so fast and we could not afford to heat our apartment, so we huddled under blankets in the cold. We fixed the chimney and lit fires in mid-winter, but even that did not heat up all the rooms. I was the only one earning, all the others were students, so it was tough.'

Sasha nudges into the conversation. 'You call that tough? You come and live with us then! When your home is made from ice and there is ice outside, you have nowhere to escape into the warmth. That is when you have to warm yourself from the inside. You dream of fires in your belly and you imagine them heating you through the layers of skin and flesh.'

'Too hard,' chips in Ellen, an Orkney storyteller. 'I'd rather a nip of peat-smoked malt whisky. My father makes the best. I'll give you some to take home, Sasha.' Sasha grins. Her own father is fond of whisky when he can get it.

Ellen raises her glass to toast the success of the festival and invites any of the storytellers to join a group planning a holiday after the performances end. Since she has use of a clutch of small seaside cottages in the Orkney Islands, off the north-east coast of Scotland, she can provide free accommodation if they are willing to share living expenses. The group cheers her hospitality and half a dozen performers can take the time off work to come. They plan to hire a van and explore the Scottish coastline, wending their way north to meet the ferry to take them across to the islands from Scrabster.

Sahara might join them later, but she has to stay to wind up the organisation and report back to the funding groups that underwrote the festival. So far, Monique from the West Indies/Germany, Sasha from the fishing village of Akranes on the west coast of Iceland, Camilla from England, Cowrie from Aotearoa/New Zealand, and Ellen from Orkney can definitely make it, along with Uretsete and DK from the Siliyik performance group. The others need more time to consider. Cowrie smiles when Sasha raises her hand. She'd like to get to know this Sealsinger much better. She likes all the others.

Except for Camilla, whose performances she missed. Word came back that Camilla was a committed Christian fundamentalist and Royalist and her version of story-telling lay in embellished tales from the mighty Empire. Cowrie's defences are likely to rise in such company and her usual hospitality runs on a much shorter string. It's possible Camilla might rethink her eagerness to be stranded on an island and outnumbered by indigenous storytellers. Then again, the point of storytelling is to develop awareness and tolerance.

Ellen drains the last drop of draught from her glass and burps loudly in appreciation. Camilla turns up her nose in absolute abhorrence and rises to pay her bill. Ellen grins, hoping her small, ungracious act of defiance may put Camilla off. Unbeknown to her, Camilla's great joy in life is converting heathens and pagans like Ellen to her path. She approaches such tasks with missionary zeal, and as she pays her bill, is already planning her tactics, gleeful that she will have the chance to examine these pagans at close range, in an island setting where they cannot escape easily.

[3]

Fire lights the night sky. From a distance, giraffes poke their heads above the bushes. Lions roar, elephants grunt and springboks leap, as the flamebearer advances, his face painted with berry juice, his eyes wide and lit from below, his ears peeled, waiting for the unexpected. In the blink of an eye, a monkey lands on his head and his spears scatter over the floor of the theatre. The other creatures, African men and women painted and prancing like the animals they mimic, roar into the audience, running away from the flame and the cries of the man. As he struggles to free himself, a lion purrs hungrily next to Sahara, on the edge of her seat in the auditorium. The theatre lights black out, leaving the audience to wonder who is victor and who is victim, after they have watched scores of hunters shoot native animals and cut off their heads as trophies, selling them to the white men who came to hunt or take back souvenirs of their extinguished manhood.

As the lights come up, the animals remain in the aisles and among the audience, to remind them they are still present, but they might not always be there. The lights fade and silently, the animals move back on stage, ready to grunt and roar and cry as the fire flames the stage for the last time and the crowds roar their appreciation back to the African storytellers and performers from Ethiopia, Kenya, South Africa and Namibia, who make up the troupe performing tonight at Theatre in the Round. As the actors crouch in their animal positions, the audience cheers and claps and stamps its feet noisily.

'This is great, Sah. I could be back home.' Cowrie

murmurs to her friend, enjoying the rowdy audience response.

After several curtain calls, the animals in different poses each time, the director comes out to explain that this troupe comprises people from many different tribes all over Africa, that there are fishermen and teachers and nurses and street people represented, that each of them brought their own stories and traditions to the theatre piece and that they still need funding to get home after the festival. Buckets are handed out to the audience and people give generously, knowing the cheap ticket prices would have barely covered the theatre hire let alone any other expenses.

Afterwards, Sahara drives Cowrie to the top of Arthur's Seat, the impressive hill sculpted like a brooding beast, which overlooks Edinburgh. They look out over the city lights and the mist appearing around the edges of the perimeter. Cowrie has never seen an ancient city with such an appealing atmosphere — haunting and yet romantic, buildings huddled together in gorgeous embrace, from Newtown to the old structures, intricately planned and beautifully orchestrated, while still pleasing to the eye. From above, the city looks almost circular, its outside buildings nurturing and encasing its heart like a living, pulsating creature.

'Could be the shell of a giant sea turtle,' whispers Sahara in Cowrie's ear.

'Not so fantastic, Sah. You know that in many Pacific myths, the islands are depicted as turtles who swam to their current destinations, then their fins were cut off, so that they would stay floating in the same place, unable to move.'

'Ugh. That's nearly as morbid as the father who cut off the fingers of his daughter that they could become seals,' replies Sahara.

'Well, yes. But we all have different ways of explaining how we came to be here, eh? I can't see that the stories from the bible are any different from these other tales, except that the bible stories have had heaps more propaganda and publicity.'

'Sure. But why did I never hear any of these other stories while growing up in England? I mean we colonised the West Indies, Australia, Africa, New Zealand, just to name a few countries, and yet we still never heard any of these alternative stories which must have been known by the colonisers.'

'Maybe, but I bet the Christian missionaries who were a vital part of the colonisation had no intention of bringing stories back home. They went to rid the heathens of these tales and replace them with their own. It was never supposed to be a two way process — until now, perhaps. I have to rethink a lot after this awesome storytelling festival. Thanks, Sah, for organising it.'

'The least I could do, as a British kid, I reckon,' laughs Sahara. 'Maybe it is my small way of righting the balance.'

'Well, we need more of it. Reckon we reach far more people by celebrating the differences than arguing over who is right.' Cowrie looks down onto a rounded building, impressive in its semi circular structure. 'What's that, Sah?'

'That's the old Scottish Parliament, before us Poms took away their government.'

'Yeah, but didn't they fight for sovereignty and get it back?'

'Yes. But people in Britain have no idea of the real issues. They just see Wales and Ireland and Scotland as a part of "Great Britain" and can't understand what all the fuss is about.'

'Too close to home, maybe? Okay to fight the battles overseas, but this is just too bloody close for comfort, eh?'

'Maybe.' Sahara moves over to the edge of Arthur's Seat. She points north. 'The Orkneys are up there. I'm glad you are going to stay with Ellen afterwards. You'll love the ruggedness of those islands.'

'Will you come up after you've finished the festival work?'

'Maybe.' Sahara grins. 'I have a reason to stay actually. You know that West Indian dancer we met the other night?'

'Yeah. Awesome dreads.'

'We've been reading poetry together at nights and there is something very special between us. Maybe I'll stay to explore it before the group leaves.'

'You old devil, Sah.' Cowrie grins. 'You kept that quiet.'

Sahara smiles. She takes Cowrie's hand. 'C'mon turtle. I want you to see something.' Together they walk over the hills along tracks and breathe in the crisp night air. Eventually, they come to a grove of trees with a small lake behind. As they approach, Sahara puts her finger to her lips. Quietly, they tiptoe to the edge of the lake and peer through the leaves. Gliding eerily across the lake are sleeping swans, their necks tucked delicately into their bodies, some under their giant wings. They watch the swans in silence for some time, hearing only the beating of their own hearts, as the Edinburgh mist gathers around them, enclosing them in a gorgeous blanket of sweet moisture.

[4]

Beneath the Orcadian waters of the Bay of Skaill, the seaweed dances, twisting her tentacles with the olivy branches of her sisters and the seals nuzzle into the deep as the wild surf pounds over their heads. They frolic and play, aware that they will be called to the surface soon, for they each must take turns to swimguard the reefs in case the Nofin humans try to invade their sacred birthing sites.

'Looks like Morrigan has begun her task. Laukia-manuikahiki says she is bringing the Nofin storytellers to our sacred Orkney Isles, that this is the place for their initiation into the Otherworld.'

'Do you think they are ready for this yet?'

'I'm not so sure, meself, but she believes it's a good place to start. At least they acknowledge there is more to our survival than merely a material existence.'

'Aye, Fiona, there's many a lass who found her ways into the sea to learn this very lesson, you included.'

Fiona scrunches up her sealy face, her whiskers twitching, then replies with a swish of her oily tail as she does a loop over the head of Sandy, as if in denial of her once human form. Sandy grins, knowing he has touched a raw nerve in his mate. For Fiona was once Nofin living on the land beside the sea. She came from a very affluent family, descended from the Viking invaders of Orkney, and lived off the riches of her elders, dispersing charity more as an extension of her churched ego than because she cared for others. Fiona never believed in anything other than a material existence, until one day, she was walking along the Bay of Skaill and a beautiful, dark man approached her. She was normally afraid of strangers, but he held a magnetic charm she could not defy. She let him come near, and he pulled her into the sea. From that day forth, she became a selkie, never wanting to return to her former life, but often wondering what had become of her family and friends. Sandy was the name of the man, and he became her mate for life.

[5]

'Oh, God, I'm about to vomit.' Camilla holds her stomach as she leans over the port side of the 'St Ola', bound from Scrabster to Orkney.

'Hang in there, Camilla. You'll be okay.' Morrigan holds her steady as Camilla's face reflects all the subtle shades of seaweed green that Morrigan has noticed in the rock pools and low tides at the Bay of Skaill.

'Stand straight and think of England,' Cowrie adds, with more than a light touch of irony in her voice. This is what they'd been taught in the British school system before kohanga reo and kura kaupapa education began. It has always seemed an appropriate expression coming from a culture that taught their colonies how to grin and bear their slavery by adopting a 'stiff upper lip'.

Camilla glares at her from behind her dark glasses. She does not like this Cowrie woman much. Too wild and arrogant and needing more discipline in her life. Nevertheless, despite herself, Camilla enjoyed Cowrie's storytelling session, though she did tend to idolise the natives a bit much for Camilla's liking. She put it down to current trendiness and was determined not to let it get in the way of a free holiday in the Orkneys. She had wanted to do that for ages, but the B&Bs were far too expensive for an island devoid of trees let alone culture. Still, it would be superb to see St Magnus Cathedral. That would make the entire trip worth putting up with some of the other storytellers less educated, in Camilla's opinion, but perhaps in need of her guidance.

'Wow, check out those awesome mountains,' yells Cowrie, against the wind blustering into them from the

16

open deck. She points to the other side of the boat as the Hoy Hills rise like a taniwha from the wild ocean crashing around them. They make their way across the swaying deck to get a closer look, Camilla following behind like a drenched sheep about to withstand another Orkney storm. The magnificent Hoy Hills erupt from the swirling ocean, their towering cliffs revealing layers of sculpted sandstone. Hidden in high crevices in the rock face are nesting fulmars with their mates gliding above them, their wings silently outstretched, letting the winds play with their flight.

'Aaargh . . . aaargh . . . aaargh . . .' Camilla vomits into the wind and the full force of her greasy 'St Ola' breakfast special, fried eggs, sausages, baked beans, chips drenched in vinegar, comes flying into the faces of the group lined along the deck. Unfortunately, it also catches the freshly dry-cleaned suit of an Orkney Islands Council Department Head who was keen to make an impression since he had won his job over a local Orcadian and knew already the task ahead would not be easy. He glares at her and takes out his handkerchief, mumbling something about people who ought to vomit into prepared bags and not over the side of boats, and especially not into a head wind. Morrigan strides towards him. 'Sorry about that, Sir. Let me help you.' She pulls off her woollen scarf and rubs the vomit deeper into his suit, giving the impression she is out to help. The man is dumbfounded, not quite realising what is happening but knowing somehow, deep inside himself, that this woman who is trying to help him is also making it worse. He pushes her away briskly.

'Lay your hands off me, young man. I am perfectly capable of cleaning myself.' With that, he strides off down the deck, rubbing his suit furiously, knowing there is not much time before he will be met by his new bosses on the pier at Stromness.

'There was no need to be so rude to him, Morrigan,' whispers Camilla, offended by her arrogance.

'Well, clean up yer own vomit then,' replies Morrigan, and heads for the cabin so she can prepare for the rush to the cars once they round the bend into the harbour. Cowrie grabs her arm before she can enter the stairwell.

'C'mon Morrigan. I know Camilla can be a pain but it never occurred to her not to vomit into the wind. She lives inland, remember.'

Morrigan grimaces. 'Bloody Poms. They're so helpless.'

'Maybe so, but let's hang out on the deck until they call us below. I want to see the village you described that you love so much.'

Morrigan returns to the deck, making sure she does not stand downwind of Camilla, and points out the Hoy lighthouse as they round the bend, and the seashore leading up to Stromness, which she says is full of fossils and relics. Out of the distant mists, the ancient town of Hamnavoe rises from the water like a whale floating towards them. Gradually, they pick out houses dotted about the hills and fishing boats along the shore. Shops and homes hang out over the harbour like they were born this way, as if an extension of the land itself. It is impossible to see where the land ends and the water begins until they sail closer to the shore. The call to return below deck comes but Cowrie cannot tear herself away from the sight. She has the strange feeling she has been here before, as if some ancient memory is stirring within her.

Morrigan leans over the edge, staring intently into the water. Cowrie glances down and notices two seals beneath them swimming alongside the boat. They are staring up at Morrigan and she looks as if she has

18

entered another world. She has not even noticed the ship's call for passengers to go below deck and collect their belongings. Cowrie nudges her, saying they should go. Morrigan cannot take her eyes from the water and the seals cannot stop swimming alongside the boat. It's as if an invisible thread connects them. Suddenly, Morrigan breaks away and heads for the stairs. As if heeding her movement, the seals dive out from the boat's side wake and head off toward the Hoy coastline.

[6]

'Eets Morrigan all right. Sandy spits out some seaweed caught in his teeth. 'Eye'd know thaat feece in a school of sharks.'

'So she wus reet then, the turtle woman. Morrigan is bringing the Pacific turtle woman back heer to see her Orkney roots then?'

'Aye, looks thaat way, Fiona. Seems leek she's een for a bitterashock.'

'Aye, yer coold be right theer, Sandy.' Fiona flicks her tail in his face, hoping to get him to dive after her and play in the swells off Hoy.

But Sandy is preoccupied. He is thinking about the consequences of too many Orcadian secrets being let loose on those who may not be ready to hear them. Coming to terms with one's past, be it communal or individual, requires preparation and a willing readiness. Otherwise things can go very wrong. He knows this well, since his own sister was told she was related to the sealpeople. It sent her right loopy and she ended up in a looney bin. She never recovered and eventually died from loneliness and isolation and perceived madness. She feared that all her family were animals, that she had lost her connection to civilisation after the disappearance of Sandy and all the rumours that abounded on the island.

She moved from the Mainland to Sanday to escape the stories, but they knew her past before she had even stepped off the boat there. She lived in an old stone cottage, knitting jumpers for tourists under a scheme launched by some enterprising women. But she was let go because no matter what the pattern that was given, she always knitted seals into the design. She could not stop herself. Finally, one of the shrinks from down south had suggested she would be better in some looney bin in the Scottish Highlands. They came and fetched her and took her away. She continued to knit seals. Her room was full of tea cosies and half-finished jumpers, scarves and socks, all with black seals swimming across them. The occupational therapists had seen wonderful progress with her work, until one day she sewed together all the knitted items and hung herself from the bed-end with them. They found her dangling from the bedpost, seals swimming around her neck and body and legs.

She had cut herself trying to remove her skin, to give it back, so that she could be free again, she had told one of the nurses. They had thought her stark raving mad the first time she cut into her flesh, and upped her pills. The lithium simply made it worse. She knitted frantically until she had the means to secure her end. Some of the other residents held a funeral service for her and they all donated stuffed seals to her memory, little realising how this would haunt her beyond the grave, be one final mocking from a world which had rejected her for her marine connections.

Sandy had never gotten over her death. He felt powerless to do anything. He loved life from the moment the seals had come to claim him back to their fold. But she could not cope with the truth and he could not reach her and tell her it was all right, that it was an honour to be related to the sealfolk, not an insult. Part of his desire to lay claim to Fiona was that he hoped she would return to the shore to convince his sister that all was well. But Fiona never wanted to do that. She felt it was best to leave things as they were. She knew only too well the difficulties of coming to terms with her destiny, and she felt it was up to Rita to make peace with her life. Sandy gradually accustomed himself to this idea, but deep inside he still felt some guilt that he could not have done more for his sister.

Fiona makes one last attempt to gain his attention by doing an eskimo roll over and around him, flicking her tail fins up his body as she passes by. Sandy flips himself into action and chases her along the coast of the Hoy Hills. Fe never liked to be away from home too long. She feared the Nuckelavee, an ancient sea monster that was said to haunt the oceans surrounding Orkney. She should know better, of course, Sandy always argued. It was simply a Nofin myth trying to make sense of an undersea world they knew too little about. But Fiona's human past always ruled her reason when it came to such issues, so he usually gave in gracefully.

As he watches her dive, he thinks how lucky he is to have won such a beautiful Nofin back to the sea. Her sleek, oily body skims the water as if she were made for this life instead of inheriting it later. Her fins fly through the waves and she swims with such skill it always holds him in awe. But it is her eyes that still captivate his heart. Deep blue and green and sometimes tawny brown, depending on the colour of the sea and the quality of the sunlight filtering through. Her eyes are knowing, intelligent, instinctive and full of tenderness, all qualities she lacked in her earthly existence.

This leads Sandy to wonder. Maybe if they willed Morrigan back into the sea, she would assume her once gentle qualities. Or would she always have to be the woman warrior, the old Queen of the Orkneys, reigning in all others to her fold?

[7]

They arrive at the cottage in the hills above the Bay of Skaill and can barely get out of Morrigan's old van, the wind is raging so harshly. The door flies back into their bodies three times before they are allowed out. But the view is worth it. The women look down into a beautiful bay, with breakers crashing into large sculpted rocks of slate and sandstone. Seaweed swirls in the swells, flinging its tentacles in the direction of each new wave, only to be flung back over its own arms again in a never-ending motion of dancing movement. To the left of the bay, a large peninsular lurches out into the sea, its headlands resembling a turtle, with a dark cave entrance showing through to the other side of the wild ocean, as if the eye in a rounded turtle head. To the right, rugged cliffs with layers of rock and ledges which the grey and cream wave-surfing fulmars have claimed for their homes.

Cowrie scans the bay, noticing a few homes and farmhouses scattered about with land around them and a small cottage right on the beach. Morrigan's home is an old stone croft, falling into ruins in places, and patched up with rusted corrugated iron she has found in abandoned building sites. It is part of a compound of dilapidated stone cottages with dry-stone walls also falling in around them and grass mixed with wildflowers, as tall as Cowrie's thighs. She steals a glance at Camilla, who looks suitably horrified. This is not exactly the free seaside B&B she had imagined when Morrigan invited them over. The cold wind bites into them and urges them forward, though the cottages hardly look welcoming.

Inside, they consist of the bare essentials. Old patches of carpet and walls different-coloured from free paint samples line them all. Some of the windows are boarded up and the saving grace is that almost every room has a fireplace. Cowrie wastes no time in asking where the wood is. Morrigan bursts into loud guffaws of laughter, barely able to contain herself. 'How many trees did you spy driving here from Stromness, Cowrie?'

'Well, I must admit, the landscape was noticeable for a lack of vegetation, apart from a few flax bushes and cabbage trees in some gardens.'

'And do flax bushes and cabbage trees strike you as good firewood?'

'Point taken, Morrigan. There's stuff all trees and what there is ain't the best firewood. So what d'ya use?'

'Peat, peat and more peat. Lucky my relatives still own cutting rights. There are spades in the garden shed and you can all come peat digging with me tomorrow.'

'Now, you really are kidding us, Morrigan. Even I know that peat has to be dried for months before using,' laughs Camilla.

'Aye, lassie,' Morrigan assumes her native tongue, 'but what yee dinnit ken is that for each bag o' peat we take, we mist ulsa cut that much for the next bugger who comes along.'

All the blood drains from Camilla's face at this point. Not only is this not the guest holiday she wanted, but she will be forced into hard labour simply to keep warm. She shudders at the thought. 'But I cannot cut peats with you. I have suffered for years from a bad back,' she whimpers.

'Well, then lassie, yee ken lift a saucepan or a tattie masher, right?' Morrigan asks, handing Camilla a pan from the rough wooden shelf with her left hand and lighting the old gas cooker with her right hand. 'The tatties lie in those mounds out there. Get Cowrie to help you dig a few tatties and turnips. I've a yen for some clapshot tonight.' With that, Morrigan turns on her heel and heads for the sea, yelling against the wind that she'll be back for dinner at six.

Cowrie and Camilla eye each other suspiciously, but realise that it may come down to a case of them versus Morrigan if push comes to shove and maybe they had better make an effort to get along now. 'She has certainly changed from the Ellen we met in Edinburgh, right?' says Cowrie.

'From the minute she told us her true name on the boat coming to Orkney, it was as if she assumed another identity,' asserts Camilla. 'And she certainly romanticised these huts we are supposed to live in. I will be checking out the B&Bs tomorrow for sure.'

'Hang on, Camilla. This is supposed to be a communal sharing of storytelling we came for. It hardly matters where we live, so long as we have a roof over our heads. I reckon these cottages will be okay once we get some fires lit. Let's get to it.'

'It's fine for you, Cowrie. You live in huts in New Zealand anyway. But I am used to a little more comfort.'

'Please yourself, Camilla. But I'm off to the beach to gather driftwood to start a fire. I spied a heap of coal in one of the sheds and that can do until we beg, borrow or steal some peats.'

'I can save you the effort. I saw some firelighters in the kitchen, so that can get us started. You dig the potatoes and turnips and I will get the fire going.' Camilla makes for the shelf and then the fireplace. Cowrie walks to the shed to look for a spade. Inside, there are oars hanging from the ceiling and she wonders where the boat is kept. Old fishing nets hang down over the windows and lobster pots are stacked up the sides. There are black bags tied at the neck which she hopes will be full of coal. She opens one to see heaps of dried cow dung piled up inside. She closes it quickly, before the whiff pollutes her nostrils. She opens another. The same. Dried shit.

Why on earth would Morrigan keep this like sacred potatoes, maturing in the shed? She tries a third bag. Dung again. The she notices one marked, 'For Kelpie'. She unties the knot and sees a note inside. 'I saved you some peats, my love. Yours, Morrigan.' The bag is again full of dung. Then it suddenly dawns on her. This must be dried peats. No wonder they don't smell too bad.

Cowrie picks up a piece and tries to crumble it in her hand. It stays solid. She holds it up to her nose and is infused with the most wonderful fragrance of wild-flowers and earth, smoked fish and the malt whisky Kuini sometimes drinks. She closes the bag for Kelpie and grabs another, determined this will be their fire tonight even if she has to cut wet peats all week to make up for it, and begins dragging it out to the door. Her elbow knocks against some garden tools and she remembers she has come in here to look for a spade.

Once she has the peats in the house, she returns for the spade. It has disappeared. She looks everywhere, but cannot locate it. She reaches for a pitch fork instead, knocking over an old chest. Its contents lie sprawled over the earth floor. Some kind of animal skin, almost like her oilskin coat. Ugh! Cowrie stuffs it back into the chest but the oil from its fur stays clinging to her hand. She wipes it down her trouser leg, grabs the pitch fork and strides down toward the tattie patch.

Morrigan watches from behind the third cottage, wondering why Cowrie is so long in her shed, thinking she must get a lock for it or dig a hole and bury the chest underground. She'd stolen back to get the spade, but Cowrie had returned again and she had to hide. Maybe it wasn't such a good idea to bring these Nofins back to Orkney after all?

[8]

'What are the raised earth mounds, like a maze, on the left hill just above the beach?' Cowrie asks, loading another serving of clapshot onto her plate.

'Skara Brae. It's a five thousand-year-old village built in the Stone Age, complete with stone furniture, hearths and drains,' Morrigan replies, her mouth full of mashed potato and turnip.

'Don't talk with your mouth full,' Camilla injects, reaching for the pepper.

Morrigan takes no notice at all and the look on Camilla's face shows she means business and will not give up until she has taught this heathen some manners. Camilla has begun to take on Morrigan as her main cause in life, as if to make up for the less than adequate accommodation, and has spent most of the afternoon cleaning up and getting the cottage into some semblance of order.

'How come it has survived that long?' asks Cowrie.

'It was buried underground until 1850 when it was uncovered by a violent storm.'

'Is it possible to see inside?'

'If you want to give money to them down south, go by day. Otherwise, locals just scale the wall from the beach at dusk and take any visitors who are fit enough to go with them.'

'I certainly will not be scaling walls by night,' replies Camilla, offended at the thought of it. 'You should be supporting Historic Scotland for preserving such sites by visiting in the conventional way.'

'Stuff the lot of them. They're from down south and are after our jobs and our money. They travel up here

28

and start bed-and-breakfasts and fancy things for tourists and then they go for the plum jobs, leaving islanders on the outer. Next thing you'll be wanting to move out of the cottage here and into one of their fancy bed-and-breakfasts.'

Camilla blanches as she had intended doing just that once she had got Morrigan sorted out and the cottage in some fit shape for her to live in. Through a face full of tatties, Cowrie grins and winks at Camilla, then decides she should rescue her from further embarrassment. 'So who lived at Skara Brae? Do they know much from the evidence of the village?'

'It comprises domestic houses with furniture like ours, only much rougher, of course, and made from stone. Some say a community of women lived there. Two old women were found buried in the walls of one of the houses and that form of interrment was only ever given to highly respected elders.'

'Fascinating. I'd love to look inside it. So amazing to see the remains of a Stone-age village right on the edge of such a wild ocean beach. Awesome.' Cowrie offers the last of the clapshot to Morrigan who takes it all, then pushes back her chair and stands, telling them she will be away for the night and not to expect her until late the next day.

Camilla and Cowrie clear up after dinner and survey their home for the next few months.

'Well, ya can't shoot through now, Camilla, after she said that,' offers Cowrie, grinning. Camilla admits it would be difficult and in any case she has a full time job ahead getting the wretched cottage in a fit state. Cowrie suggests that she should stay and keep an eye on Morrigan and do just that while she tackles the second cottage in preparation for Sasha and Monique to come. She wants to make sure that she will at least be in the same house as Sasha to get to know her better. It's still possible that DK and Uretsete, now lovers, will join them later after they have travelled up through Scotland and visited Iona, which Uretsete was keen to do, so they can have the third cottage. 'How do you know DK and Uret — whatever her name is?' asks Camilla.

'Both were students when I was teaching while completing my doctorate at the University of California in Berkeley. DK was the young radical and Uretsete was niece of my lover, Peta.'

'You never struck me at the festival as a doctoral type,' admits Camilla.

'So what's a doctoral type? We don't play into all that Oxford and Cambridge upper class crap back home. It simply means, in my case, you have a passion for words which you want to pursue with further reading.'

'Yes, but you need intelligence and perseverance to complete the work, Cowrie.'

'So you don't reckon I have those qualities, eh, Camilla?'

Camilla blanches, then her face reddens. 'I didn't say that, Cowrie.'

'You didn't need to. It was written all over your face,' retorts Cowrie, with a grin. 'C'mon Camilla, it's no big deal. I recall touring once doing readings and two twinset and pearls ladies from the bookstore in Palmerston North came to collect me. They expected some kind of bespectacled touring author with a PhD and they got a wild Hawai'ian Maori in jandals. I walked right by them to see if they would pick me. There were only eight of us disembarking from the plane. I sauntered past them, went to the loo, buggered about a bit buying postcards and collecting bags, then decided I would put them out of their misery, so I bowled up and introduced myself. D'ya know what they said? "But you don't look like a doctor". By which they meant not thin, tall, intellectual airs and pakeha.'

'What's pakeha?'

'White, euro, brit, you know, pale-face.'

Camilla blanches again. 'Well, it's true. You don't look like a doctor.'

Cowrie gives up in disgust and changes the topic, asking Camilla if she would be interested in finding out more about the Stone-age village of Skara Brae and suggesting they visit the place sometime. Camilla agrees it would be very educational and besides, she has a visitor's pass to all British and Scottish castles and monuments administered by Historic England and Scotland.

'No wonder you didn't want to scale the wall,' exclaims Cowrie. 'You crafty old witch, Camilla.'

Camilla drops the cup she is drying. It crashes onto the floor, shattering into several pieces. She faces Cowrie front on, assertively. 'Do not ever, ever, ever call me a witch. That is no joke. It is evil and heathen.'

Oh, no. She's some kind of Christian fundamentalist, thinks Cowrie, amazed at her reaction. She considers telling Camilla that witches were merely wise women whose knowledge the societal leaders wanted to silence, then realises this debate could take them into the wee hours and she is very tired after the long journey up from Scrabster. Safer to change the subject. 'Okay, so where do you think Morrigan is all night?'

'Are you suggesting she is a witch?' asks Camilla incredulously.

'No. More like she has a lover.' Cowrie remembers the message to Kelpie written on the note inside the bag of peats.

'Nobody would sleep with anybody this untidy,' asserts Camilla, picking up the shattered china and dusting the top of the fridge with the edge of her tea towel.

'Then that's settled. I'm off to bed and I assume you are happy to sleep here alone tonight in Morrigan's cottage?'

'I'm certainly not afraid of ghosts, if that's what you mean.'

Bloody ghost would be afraid of you, thinks Cowrie, smiling to Camilla and suggesting she lock the door once Cowrie has left. As she heads out into the night breeze, she hears the lock crunch down and furniture sliding across the floor. She is not sure whether Camilla is keeping her or the witches at bay. Maybe, to Camilla, they are one and the same.

Cowrie walks across the stoney earth, noticing that it is still light at half-past-nine and the sun is setting over the sea, sending an orange-pink glow into the sky above the dense layer of clouds. The billowy shapes hovering on the horizon depict a seahorse, a kina, a whale and a seal. Another patch of clouds shows a witch riding a broom. She hopes Camilla is looking out the window and is suitably impressed. In the foreground, one of the standing stones on the farm nearby suddenly starts to move. It walks with a determined stride. She could swear it was Morrigan, but Morrigan has been gone too long to be that close by. Cowrie dismisses the thought and opens the door of her cottage to find a wildcat has sprayed all over the floor. She considers returning to Camilla, but decides the cat pee is worth the freedom. Even the lumpy old mattress looks inviting when this tired. She leaps onto the mattress, fully clothed, and is asleep within minutes.

[9]

A rusted spade, its handle broken and a box of old farm implements are held up for all to see. 'Tenner, g'me a tenner. Five, a fiver. Two. Two pounds for the box lot.' A fellow in the front row with a fag hanging out his mouth and clothes that are glued to his body with soot, raises one eyebrow. 'Three. I have three quid. Goin, going, gone for three quid, to Squiddy Lamefoot.' The auctioneer's hammer goes down on the table and a red-faced man in blue overalls hands the man a ticket to claim his prize. 'Good on yer, Squiddy. Bloody nice hoe in there,' he mumbles and winks. Squiddy Lamefoot nods in reply and eyes the next lot being wheeled into the arena. It is a beautifully carved desk and a murmur of interest ripples through the room. Bids start at only five pounds, but an antique dealer from down south raises the odds and it eventually goes for eighty pounds. 'Bloody rip-off. Would've been a goner for forty had the pom not been there,' mumbles Morrigan.

'Reckon so,' agrees Cowrie. Then the wardrobe and dresser they have been waiting for is trundled in.

'Number 263, wardrobe and dresser. Open her up Timmy.' The auctioneer gestures to Timmy, who holds the long cabinet with one arm and reaches around to prise open the door with the other. It creaks, groans, then falls off with a loud thud to the floor. Collective laughter. The auctioneer manages to keep a straight face for a few seconds, then grins. 'Who'll give a tenner, a tenner for both, and I'll throw the door in for free.' More laughter. 'All right, a fiver, a fiver. Who'll give a fiver?' Cowrie begins to raise her hand but Morrigan grabs her wrist and holds it down. 'Two quid. A quid each for the dresser and the wardrobe.' The silence is unbearable. The auctioneer is about to order the goods off stage when he suddenly notices a bid. 'Two quid. Gone for two quid!' His hammer crashes onto the table in relief, and Blue Overalls approaches them, handing a ticket to Morrigan.

'How on earth did you do that?' asks Cowrie.

'It's the nose,' laughs Morrigan, twitching her nose like a seal.

'But how did he know you were bidding and it wasn't just an itch?'

'Takes one to know one,' is all Morrigan says, and she gestures Cowrie to move toward the door.

'But it isn't finished yet. What about the old lamps and carpet you liked,' pleads Cowrie, loving the energy of the auction and the people watching.

'Got to beat the rush to lunch,' winks Morrigan, leading her toward the cafeteria. Inside, a few people from the auction are already lined up for their baked tatties, pies, chips, haggis and baked beans. Cowrie watches in amazement as Morrigan orders the Auction Special and her plate is piled high with sausages, eggs, chips, baked beans and a mince laden roll on top. The cafeteria waitress then pours on half-a-cup of sweetened tomato sauce and Morrigan nods, as if they are talking in a silent code, and she squeezes mustard from a tube like toothpaste, in a swirling motion, onto the tomato sauce mixture. Pleased with her effort, she hands it over to Morrigan, 'enjoy it, love', then yells out 'next' to Cowrie. Still intrigued, Cowrie orders a salmon sand-wich, and is shocked to find it is tinned salmon, here in the land of oak-smoked fresh-caught Orkney salmon, famous throughout Scotland, nay the world if you believe the brochures put out by the local tourist board.

Morrigan nudges her to the cashier. 'No complaints, stranger. This is the Kirkwall Auction, not the bloody Savoy Hotel.' With that, Morrigan hands over a few quid and gestures them to a table in the corner where the smoke will not be so bad. There they discuss the morning's deals and what they intend to bid for in the afternoon, with Morrigan stipulating that they must never go above a fiver for anything and that if they stay silent long enough on items of interest to few others, they will walk off with a truck load of furniture, enough to make the cottages habitable.

Cowrie waits for a suitable lull in the conversation. 'Morrigan, how come you are always gone at night? Do you have a secret lover or something?'

Morrigan shifts uncomfortably in her seat, as if she has been waiting for this question. 'Not that it's any of your bloody business, but I am a fisher by night. I own a dory with a fellow in Finstown. I didn't buy the cottages on the giro, you know.'

'The giro?'

'The unemployment benefit. We lay the lobster and crab creels by night and collect them again the next night. Allows for time in the day to write and think. I like that.'

'I loved your stories at the festival. But it must be hard work fishing by night and writing by day?'

'I spend as much time thinking as writing. And talking to some of the folk around the island. They're full of stories handed down within families and parishes. Takes some time and a lot of oatcakes and strong tea to get all the details from them, but it's extraordinary what comes out sometimes.'

'Such as?'

Morrigan gets a distant look in her eye, pushes away

her plate, and leans toward Cowrie. 'You know the peedie steward on the 'St Ola' when we sailed over?'

'The short one with the dark hair and dark eyes, who Camilla thought was Italian?'

'Aye. He's descended from the selkie folk. His ancestors were seals and it is said that he inherited their skills. You should see the way he swims. I've watched him at nights in the Stromness Pool. Looks like he has fins. And he dives under with his back feet together, pushing up and down, more like a seal pup than a peedie person.'

'You're kidding me, right?' Cowrie looks into her eyes, but sees no trace of humour. Morrigan pulls out a pipe, fills it carefully, then lights up. Clearly she's chosen the non-smoking area for Cowrie, but now has invaded it herself. Cowrie does not protest, since she is more interested in finding out more about the sealfolk. But Morrigan is not to be budged.

'That's what I was told. Believe it or not. Folk around here are divided into the believers and non-believers. Maybe it's all myth.' She sucks air into her pipe and blows the smoke out again, idly making rings with her mouth.

Before Cowrie can pin her down again, the bell rings and everyone pours back into the auction rooms for a smokey afternoon of heavy bidding and concentrated energy. Between bids, Cowrie wonders how come Morrigan saw the peedie man from the boat swimming in the pool at night if she is always out fishing. She likes Morrigan, despite her gruffness at times, but something is still strange about her, inconsistent, like she is covering up for someone, maybe herself.

By the end of the day, they have accumulated enough furniture to make do in the other cottages. Morrigan explains that she and her partner will collect it from the auction rooms with his trailer before they go fishing tonight and drop it off at the cottage for Cowrie and Camilla to arrange how they please. So Kelpie is a man, Cowrie reasons, disappointed since Morrigan had always struck her as a butch dyke with her sideburns and barber shop haircut, her tweed cap perched back on her head. Or maybe, thinks Cowrie, amused, maybe he is a seal with a name like that. She chuckles to herself as they head home in the van with a few box loads of kitchen goods bought for fifty pence each.

They take the Orphir Road back from Kirkwall, and Morrigan makes a detour to collect some food for dinner. They arrive at a cliff edge covered in beautiful wildflowers and herbs like thrift and sorrel sprouting amidst the wind-blown heather and looking down over a sandy bay where the tide goes out for miles. Morrigan collects bags from the back of the van and hands Cowrie a knife, beckoning her to follow the cliff path down to the beach. Cowrie asks what the knife is for. All she can hear back through the blustering wind is 'spoots'. What the hell are spoots, she wonders, marching behind Morrigan in her gumboots and oilskin. Morrigan needs neither for protection. It's as if she was born in the sea.

[10]

'Urgh. How uncivilised!' Camilla rolls her eyes in disgust as the white penis-like erection slithers towards her on the rack. It hisses at her, sending out a spray of salt water, then withdraws into its shell to prepare for another attack, until it begins to sizzle over the peat fire and finally give up its last struggle for survival. Even Cowrie, who loves shellfish, feels uncomfortable about cooking it alive.

'You're hypocritical wimps. You'll eat smoked farmed salmon and packaged lamb which has led a miserable life fenced into wind-blown pastures, force-fed then taken to the slaughterhouse to be hacked into pieces with a chainsaw, but you can't look at spoots cooked over a fire. The only difference is that you don't see the fish being caught and processed and the lambs being murdered and because you don't see it, you don't think about it.' Morrigan has a swig of Scapa from one glass and a swig of Highland Park from another. 'Think I'll settle for the Scapa tonight,' she admits. 'Those buggers at Highland Park are a bit smooth for my liking, though their single malt is damned hard to beat. She pours another glass, swills it around in her hand, and downs it in one go. 'That'll keep me warm for the fish tonight,' she grins, laughing to herself.

Camilla starts into a debate on the relative merits of fish, meat and vegetarianism, blaming radical activists and Oprah Winfrey for the downturn in beef sales due to BSE in the UK. Morrigan argues with her and Cowrie concentrates on the spoots opening their shells and revealing their beautiful fleshy bodies sizzling in succulent seawater. What an extraordinary experience, walking backwards over the sands at Waulkmill Bay to trick the spoots into thinking you were leaving rather than coming, then plunging a knife into the hole and attempting to pull them up before they burrow deeper into the sand. She and Morrigan had a hilarious time battling it out with the razor fish, known locally as spoots, and for each one caught, at least three more dived their way to freedom. She doesn't feel quite so bad knowing this, but Morrigan has a worthwhile point too.

By now, Camilla has worked herself into a eulogy of protection for the poor fox hunters of England who may be privileged enough to own mansions and horses and packs of dogs and pretty clothes, but they are wickedly attacked by those misguided animal activists who are probably Greens or Lib Dems in disguise anyway, if not New Labour, the way they are behaving. Cowrie interrupts their argument, which is leading nowhere fast but simply reinforcing their own intractable positions, by sliding spoots onto their plates, shell and all. Camilla is distracted by the black and brown intestines and threatens to be sick. That is enough to make Morrigan remove the plate, having experienced this before, and cut off the lower part of the spoots, leaving only the tops. Once Camilla tastes the scallop-like flavour, shutting her eyes against the memory of their live wriggling bodies, she is hooked and asks if next time they could buy them frozen to avoid seeing them die. At this point, Morrigan rolls her eyes, wondering if she had been heard at all by Camilla, and prepares to depart for her night duty.

'I'll be back soon with the auction furniture so you lovely ladies can amuse yourself tonight while I'm out fishing. No fighting now.' She grins, clamps down her cap, and marches down to the van, yelling back, 'Thanks for the barbecue, Cowrie. Next time, make sure there are more tatties!' The stones fly out from under her wheels as she takes off with a roar, leaving Cowrie and Camilla, as usual, to clear up and do the dishes.

'How do you think she coped before we came?' asks Camilla, picking up the plates.

'I reckon she ate from one bowl and had very simple food. Look at her kitchen. It's a bachelor pad.'

'She needs a good woman to take care of her,' asserts Camilla, wiping clean the outside table.

Maybe you, thinks Cowrie, loving the idea of these two stuck in the cottage forever debating the issues of existence. Until this moment, it had never occurred to her that it may be Camilla and not Morrigan who is the closet dyke after all.

When they have finished the dishes, Morrigan returns in a large truck loaded up with the furniture, and three chaps to help unload it, Billy, Pete and Squiddy. Cowrie recognises the man from the auction who got the farm equipment, but he never even raises an eyebrow to her now. They unload and are back in the truck heading for the harbour to load up their boats for the night's fishing. No Kelpie, as Cowrie had expected. The mystery remains. She cannot imagine he could be one of these fellows. Then again, with Morrigan, you never can tell.

[11]

'She's coming oot to see us tonight, Fiona. I can feel it in my bones. She'll tell us why they are here and what they want from us.'

Fiona munches on a kelpy branch swinging in the surf, not much concerned about what the Nofins want or do not want. She is relieved to be free of them, at last, and has no desire to return to the confines of the house of Skaill where she was imprisoned in the feudal system of domestic slavery and a prisoner to expectations and outward shows of manners and etiquette.

Sandy swims near her, sensing her reluctance and fins gently up her side, along her belly, down to her tail fins. Fiona shudders with delight, swings around and fins him under his chin. They nuzzle and play and swim away again.

'I think the time has come to share our knowledge. Morrigan has told us this. She always predicted this day would arrive. But I'm not sure yee're ready for it, Fe.' Sandy looks her closely in the eyes. Fiona can never resist this from him. She eyes him back, finning the water around her, sending a fleshy, succulent seaweed branch floating towards him. Sandy smiles, knowing she can always distract him, especially when she is not ready to answer or commit herself to any action.

'I just hope Morrigan knows what she is letting herself in for. Releasing knowledge too soon is as bad as never at all.' Sandy notices a longfin cruising nearby and nudges Fiona into the shadows of the thick forest of kelp that lines the rock ledges until he has passed on.

Soon, a whirring through the waters. Then silence.

A dark oval shape glides above them, floating on the surface, lapping in the swell. A crashing sound as a huge crate breaks the surface of the sea, then slowly sinks down past them, weighted by lead sinkers and lands on the rocky floor, baited and inviting fat lobsters to crawl inside. Then a splash, as something larger hits the waves, huge fins first and body after. Is it her, is it Morrigan, come to see them?

[12]

Finally the day has arrived. The big bird whirrs in from the skies above Kirkwall and lands in forty-knot winds despite all odds. Cowrie's heart beats as the passengers disembark. No Monique, no Sasha. Then they appear from behind a burly man. After them, a sweet young couple holding hands. As they approach, Cowrie recognises it is DK and Uretsete following behind and she rushes toward them in glee, glad that she and Camilla have had time to prepare the cottages since both groups have now arrived together.

After greetings all round, and baggage collecting, Cowrie guides them towards the van which Morrigan let her borrow for the day. They pile in, eager to tell her about their adventures in Scotland after the Edinburgh Festival. Monique and Sasha drove through the Highlands, stopping off at various points to tramp in the heather and peats and DK and Uretsete took a bus and boat to Mull and then to Iona and had 'amazing mystical experiences' according to DK. Cowrie laughs, thinking how the younger DK she first met would have scoffed at such an idea, and how her relationship with Uretsete has changed her. They fight to be first to tell their stories, but it is a relief to be with their bubbling energy after the more dour and constrained company of Morrigan and Camilla.

They drive through Finstown and Cowrie notices the fishing dory, 'Selkie Too', part-owned by Morrigan, is not back in port yet. It is now 10 a.m. and way past the time Morrigan usually ties up. She stops at Seafayre and takes them into the large seaside barn where thousands of fresh scallops, oysters, cockles, mussels and spoots lie in freshly piped seawater, waiting to be exported. The young woman hosing down the shellfish recognises Cowrie and waves. She approaches and asks what they want. Cowrie tells them to choose what they'd like for dinner and they can later cook it over the peat fire. As they point out the most appealing crustaceans, the woman wades into the pools in her gumboots and picks out the chosen shellfish with a net. They cannot believe their eyes at the luxury of such fresh seafood at such a reasonable cost. Nor could Cowrie, the day Morrigan brought her in here and introduced her to Shelley. They pay in cash and depart, the van full of luscious kai moana.

Uretsete and DK are waxing lyrical about the awesome beauty of Iona and the wonderful tales they heard from the locals about the island, weaving their impressions of nature and the inner stories of the island history and folktales into an appetising whole. All the while, Sasha listens with interest as Cowrie watches her through the rear vision mirror. At one point, Sasha catches her eye and winks. Cowrie winks back. There is such humour and beauty in this woman, such energy. Cowrie is transported into the theatre where Sasha first performed her Inuit stories, and she especially loved the tale of the seals. Suddenly, a truck nearly edges them off the road. Cowrie had allowed her concentration to lapse a moment and they narrowly avoid a deep ditch. Looking back in the mirror, Cowrie sees not Sasha, but the back of Morrigan's head as she whooshes by. She could swear it was the same truck that delivered the furniture. So how come Morrigan's dory had not yet returned? 'Hey, watch the road, Prof,' DK warns, grinning. Cowrie returns to the present, murmuring an apology to the group and soon the talk returns to their journeys.

By the time they arrive at the Bay of Skaill, Morrigan is sitting at the table with Camilla, tucking into a hearty brunch of baked beans and fried eggs, oatcakes and tea, looking like she has been there for hours. She greets them with energy and says Cowrie will show them to their accommodation. The women are charmed by the cottages, not noticing the leaks and ruined walls, so good has been the renovation work. Curtains from the auction, found crumpled in the bottom of boxes bought for fifty pence, cover the worst. They pile their bags onto auction beds, none more than two pounds each and a bunk for three quid, and hungrily eye the shellfish, asking Cowrie when the peat fire is to be started and why they have to wait for dinner. Camilla diverts them with Westray shortbread, Orkney fudge and a huge pot of tea made from water constantly boiling on the old coal range. They settle for baked beans as a second course, agreeing to wait for the shellfish feast this evening.

Later, Cowrie asks Camilla when Morrigan arrived. She replies that she was dropped off at the gate only a short time before Cowrie returned with the others and asked her to whip up a breakfast as soon as possible since she was craving food. Camilla, glad to be of help, did so. Cowrie grills her as to the vehicle that dropped Morrigan off, but Camilla only heard it, though she says it's possible it was a truck. She still cannot figure out how come the dory was not tied up. Maybe it's in for a repair. Morrigan said it had a few leaks and would have to be fixed soon. It's pointless worrying anyway. Clearly Morrigan has her life sorted, and Cowrie would rather think about Sasha now.

The rest of the day is spent walking around the Bay of

Skaill, over the rocks to see the fulmars nesting in amongst the pink thrift high up in the cliffs opposite Skara Brae, which Cowrie is still waiting to visit. The fulmars resemble lusciously fat seagulls with their cream breasts and grey wings merging into the rocky ledges. The rocks are sculpted with lava flow lines, wind and sea-carved sandstone, forming shapes that most artists would yearn to create. The pied oystercatchers, locally known as shaldro, shriek and scream in high-pitched calls when they go anywhere near their young, nesting in amongst the small rocky caves and ledges. Seaweed swirls in the tide, large leathery strands floating on the surface, and Skara Brae still calls to them from the banks on the other side of the bay.

In the evening, they light a peat fire and roast their seafood over the grate, marvelling at the earthy, rich taste of the peat smoking through the food. Morrigan provides a sampling of peat-soaked single malt whiskies of various ages and for the first time since their arrival, she takes the night off and is relaxed. Maybe it is just the strain of battling the harsh seas and winds off Orkney to fish that makes her so surly at times, thinks Cowrie, ashamed she has ever doubted Morrigan.

Out in the bay, the seals float amongst the kelp, wailing in vain. For tonight, she'll not be coming, no matter how long they wait for her. Their heads bob up and down as the swells rise and fall, and they glance over to Skara Brae, then up the slopes towards the cottages. Smoke rises from the roof and laughter rebounds off the walls. They look intently at each other. It is a time for celebration. The women of Skara Brae have finally returned.

46

[13]

Sixteen small black dots floating on the gentle, large swell suddenly decide to take flight as they near the top of the cliff. They wheel around and over the rocks and soar up towards the cliff edge. Flashes of black and white, orange beaks and legs. The puffins pass so close they almost touch the noses of the onlookers, then one by one they each return to their mate nesting in the rocky crags on the seaward side of the Brough of Birsay. Cowrie and Sasha dangle their legs over the towering ledges, the full force of the wind in their faces and shout with glee. Fulmars with outstretched wings, glide as if surfing on the wind, almost touching the tufts of pink thrift poking out from the rocky outcrops as they sail past. One scoops over Sasha's head, forcing her to duck down and it looks back, as if pleased with its swift flight and skilful negotiation of the humans. Below, the surf throws itself onto the sandstone and rolls up the sides of the brough to gather speed to tumble down again, taking seaweed, rocks and stones back with it.

Today is glorious, the first sunny, warm day since they arrived. The initial week of settling in had its traumas once the excitement wore off, but things have now turned out well. Cowrie, Sasha and Monique are in one cottage, DK and Uretsete in the other and Camilla has stayed with Morrigan to keep house. She sees it her role to make sure Morrigan is looked after and Morrigan enjoys being waited on, so their strange union works well, so long as they keep off political issues. Sasha and Monique enjoyed travelling together through Scotland, but Monique wants to take time out for her other great passion — photography — leaving Cowrie and Sasha to explore the archeological sites and beaches while DK and Uretsete are meditating in isolated places, easy to find in Orkney.

Bobbing on the water below are some common seals, a few floating, some diving and others frolicking in the seaweed. Cowrie and Sasha watch, entranced.

'I wouldn't mind joining them if it wasn't so damn cold in the water here,' Cowrie says, nodding toward the seals.

'Cold? What a joke! This is at least twenty degrees celsius above what we endure before we begin saying it's cold.' Sasha laughs, her voice blowing back on the wind.

Cowrie grins, admitting it's all a matter of degree. She pours more ginger and honey tea from the flask they have bought with them and hands a cup to Sasha, who flashes her dark lashes in thanks and returns her gaze to the puffins nesting below them. Cowrie pours herself a cup and uses it to warm her hands. The sun here is always cancelled out by the wind, no matter how strong it is, but the views are breathtaking and more than make up for the lack of warmth. Especially now Sasha is here. Last night they stayed up much longer than the others, keeping the peat fire burning and talking intensely and intimately. They hatched a plan to visit the Brough of Birsay, checked the tides, and set out at dawn leaving a note for the others. They parked opposite the island and walked across the causeway, surrounded by magnificent species of seaweed — light to dark green, red, pink, brown and from long, thick leathery branches to small, delicate bright green sea lettuces with ferny fronds and waving arms in the rock pools.

At the other side, they scaled the rocks to the Viking and Pictish settlement ruins then kept climbing until they reached the peak of the brough where they now sit watching the puffins and fulmars.

Below them, a large dorsal fin steals through the waves and suddenly there is a wild splashing as an orca whale grabs one of the young seals and flicks it up into the air. Cowrie grabs Sasha's arm. 'Look at that. The whale is playing with the seal pup in preparation for the kill.' The other seals scatter in all directions then regroup further inland where the whale is unlikely to swim. One seal stays nearby, watching in terror, as her offspring is about to be devoured. Near the end, she swims away, defeated.

'It's life, Cowrie. Out in the kayaks, we see that almost daily back home. It's hard to find food in the arctic region and anywhere snow and ice are plentiful, so the whales take what they can, when they can. But unlike us humans, they never kill more than they can eat, despite the fact that they have ready-made freezers to store food in our land.' Sasha chuckles at the thought.

'You know that story you told about the seals at the festival? Well, do you reckon there are such people as sealfolk or is this just myth?'

Sasha turns to face Cowrie, smiling. 'There is no doubt in my mind and heart that the sealfolk did and do still exist. Remember, we are used to seeing life at surface level, literally and metaphorically. But our elders saw into people. They saw us from the inner out, rather than the outer in. And they made stories from what they saw inside us. These stories have an inner truth and wisdom. They are there for a purpose, to remind us of why we are here and what we are here for.' Sasha reaches for a salmon sandwich. Just as she brings it to her lips, a fulmar skims past and steals the bread from her hand. She laughs wildly. 'Go for it, Fulmar. Good shot!' and sticks her arm into the basket for another, still grinning at the wild audacity of the gliding bird. Cowrie smiles, loving her connectedness to nature, her instinctual responses. Suddenly Sasha starts flinging the sandwiches off the cliff and fulmars dive, catching them mid-flight and taking them back to their nests to share with their lifelong mates. Cowrie adores this, despite it being her share of the salmon flying off the cliff edge.

'Hey Sasha, that's my brunch. You'll pay dearly for this.'

'What's the currency, Cowrie? Not in pounds I hope. They are beyond my Inuit pocket.'

Without thinking, Cowrie replies, 'No. In hugs and kisses.' Before she has a chance to withdraw or cover over her slip, Sasha grabs her, bends her gently back onto the blanket and kisses her slowly, deliciously, unexpectedly. The wind tries to tip them off balance, but Sasha digs her foot into the rock ledge and braces herself while working her tongue around the edges of Cowrie's mouth then out again and over the lips, only to dive back in, like a seal playing in a sea cave. They kiss, gently, delicately, lusciously as the waves pound against the rocks below and the fulmars shriek in delight from the air above. They enter into that sensuous dreamworld for those who savour the imagery of touch.

In the distance, a floating iceberg. The sea is sleek and calm, deep green with slashes of blue. A rainbow plunges from the sky into the water beside the iceberg and a dolphin rises up next to the kayak, nudging the skin sides of the craft, her fin touching Cowrie's arm dangling near the water. She looks into the eyes of the dolphin, so gentle, wise, clear, intimate. It is Peta. The eyes dissolve into those of Sasha. She feels the tongue of the dolphin on hers.

'Cowrie, are you okay?' Sasha bends her face over her friend, who seems lost in another world, her brilliant eyes soaking sensuously through Cowrie.

'Ae. I'm okay, I think.' Cowrie rises from the deep, meeting Sasha's gaze fully. 'You took me by surprise, sent me diving into the dreamspace.'

'Oh, yeah, and I was a dolphin kissing you, right?' Sasha grins.

'How did you know that?'

'I'm descended from dolphins, and I know I've been sent to you for some reason. Right now, kissing seems a good enough excuse to find out why.' Sasha smiles. 'Besides, I have wanted to do that ever since we met at that sunny, outdoor seafood restaurant off Royal Mile in Edinburgh. I remember wanting to take you away swimming with me, but you seemed to be with Sahara, so I held back.' Sasha leans her head on her hand, lying beside Cowrie with her other hand stroking Cowrie's face.

'I was in love with Sahara, and I still love her. But she is in love with a West Indian dancer, and after our time in the Antarctic, we came to realise we had differing needs.' Cowrie kisses Sasha's hand. 'I also felt a surge of energy with you, first in the performance and then at the cafe, but then when you talked of travelling through Scotland with Monique, I wondered if you were going to be lovers.'

Sasha laughs into the wind. 'Monique, as gorgeous as she is, has a male Afro-German lover back in Frankfurt, and a child he is looking after while she is away. They both work together at the African-German Culture Cafe and organise readings and support for other Afro-Germans.'

51

'So, you'd've been tempted but for that, like me with Sahara?'

'Yes. Who wouldn't with a passionate woman like Monique, so devoted to her work. But remember, sweet Turtle, you were my first choice.' Sasha breathes hot air into Cowrie's neck which is getting cold with the wind.

'Oh, never let that stop,' moans Cowrie, enjoying the sensation. 'Hey, how come you called me turtle just then?'

'I attended all your storytelling sessions in Edinburgh and if you are not a turtle, then I am not a dolphin!' Sasha laughs, prodding Cowrie's arms. 'Look, wee fins, cute wee fins.' She starts moving them in a swimming motion and they nearly topple off the cliff edge.

'Steady on, dancing dolphin. You just about had us in the water, and I doubt even we would have survived a fall that vast.' Cowrie edges her body further from the cliff edge, Sasha moving with her, as if they are one creature crawling toward the pink thrift tufting its way through the rock crevices. They find themselves in a small grassy hollow, sheltered from the strength of the wind, and continue exploring their tongued caves in the cathedral of nature, high up from the crashing sea and far away from human interference, with only the fulmars and puffins flying over them, uttering calls of ecstacy and gliding down to tell their mates. Into the dreamworld they enter fully, aware that each of them touches the other, literally and imaginatively, as if one soaring entity, where each touch sends sensuous waves of energy flying through the other, reaches parts of them that no other human ever has.

When they surface, they stay in silence for some time, drinking in the gaze of the other. Cowrie is reminded so much of Peta, her Chumash lover on Great Turtle Island.

It's almost as if Peta has come to her in the form of Sasha. She recalls dreams of Peta falling from the Rainbow Bridge created by Hutash, and turning into a dolphin, swimming off to be with her new lover, Nanduye. Nature has rewarded her by sending back another dolphin lover in the form of Sasha, one whose lips speak of other lands and of stories and seas that Cowrie longs to explore.

'Calling all turtles. Dolphin to Turtle. Please tune in. The causeway we walked to get here at low tide is now covered in water. Are you ready to swim home with the blanket and thermos and binoculars?' Sasha points down behind them to the far side of the brough. Sure enough, the tide has turned and the walkway is covered by at least three feet of water. They quickly gather together their picnic brunch, stuff it into their backpacks, and gallop down the slopes they'd climbed so slowly before. They wave to the Norse ruins as they pass by and splash onto the walkway to find the tide is up to their waists and surging in fast.

From the other shore, people look on anxiously at the two people stranded on the island. But when the women dive into the sea, clothes, backpacks and all, a wave of shock enters them. Few Orcadians swim in local waters since they are so cold, and fewer fully clothed. But these two fin their way to the beach skilfully between the oncoming waves, as if they were used to the water. 'Must be ferryloopers,' says one man to his wife. 'No Orcadian would do that unless they were about to miss their clapshot for tea.' His wife smiles, admiring the strength and audacity of the women, wishing she could be with them instead of returning home to cook tatties for eight hungry mouths.

[14]

By the time they get home, DK and Uretsete have the peat fire going and two whole oak-smoked salmon stuffed with fresh herbs ready. Monique is still at Skara Brae taking photographs and Camilla and Morrigan are at Finstown working on cleaning the boat. The four of them settle around the fire for feasting and talkstory. Uretsete has made some corn bread and Cowrie has not tasted any so good since Peta's recipe which she often did for a treat. It seems right to share such bread tonight. DK and Uretsete are so excited by their day that they do not at first notice the new layers of intimacy between Sasha and Cowrie.

Between the cornbread laden with Orkney butter and delicious Swanney cheese, the oak-smoked salmon dripping with moisture as it cooks over the peat fire and a salad made from lettuce and fresh herbs, DK and Uretsete fill Cowrie in on the progress made by their performing talkstory group, Siliyik, representing a range of cultures from Great Turtle Island. The young students had been the talk of the fringe festival alongside Sasha's work, and they revelled in the feedback from the audiences. Most have now flown home to study but DK and Uretsete planned to do a working holiday after the festival and when the Orkney invitation came from Ellen, oops, Morrigan, as DK finds it hard to remember now, they jumped at the chance.

'Today we walked through Binscarth Wood. We'd been told Orkney had no trees, but it turns out this woodland was planted by some dudes in the nineteenth century. Cool!' DK downs some mineral water and takes a breath. 'There were bluebells and all sorts of birds I'd never, like never, seen before. Awesome!'

'Then,' continues Uretsete, 'we went to Finstown. We saw Morrigan and Camilla at the Pomona Inn where we stopped for lunch. I think Camilla was a bit drunk. She was swaying about and she was much less uptight than usual. Anyway, we wandered about the shoreline and met up with Shelley, you know, that cute woman who sold us all the fresh shellfish the day we arrived? It was her break and we shared some mineral water with her. She told us she'd been born on the island and had lived in Finstown all her life. Her dad was a fisherman named Kelpie. Anyway, one day he never returned from fishing and they found his boat drifting later, as if he'd dived overboard. His wife was despondent, took to the bottle and disappeared within a year of his going. Some reckoned he had been taken so fast that the seals had come to drag him back into the sea and she missed him so much she went to join him. Anyway, nobody has ever found either of their bodies. Shelley was adopted by her grandmother and stayed in Finstown despite all the gossip. The kids at school called her Sealface. She tried her hand at typing and waitressing at the Pomona Inn, but always felt the call of the sea. Eventually, she was offered the job at Seafayre and that suited her fine because she was returned to the fishing industry and life she grew up with. Sometimes, she says, she hears her father's voice on the wind, as if he is calling to her. She doesn't get too near the water now and never goes out on the boats in case she gets pulled in to join the seals. Amazing, eh?'

'I reckon she's at least one sausage short of a barbecue. If you ask me there's some fantasy going on there,' admits DK.

'Don't be too sure, DK,' warns Sasha, finishing a mouth full of salmon. 'These stories are not so strange in Orcadian or Hebridean waters. There's more than a few people related to the seals.'

'Yeah, but most are fantasy, right? I mean, like, you'd have to have a few screws loose to really think a seal could pull a human into the water and he could grow gills and live there.' DK pulls the fin off her salmon and throws it into the fire.

'It isn't that literal, but seals have a way of charming people and come when humans most need them. I'd give the story a little more respect if I were you.' Sasha chews the last piece of the fish and the tail pokes out of her mouth as she moves her jaws up and down, up and down. DK cannot help noticing that she looks like a seal munching on a fish in the water. She has to suppress her mirth.

'But weren't most of the seal stories about guys who stole and hid the skins of their selkie wives and thus prevented them from returning to the water? I heard several variations on that in the Scottish storytelling sessions at the festival.' DK tries to dislodge a bone from between her teeth, but is having trouble budging it.

'That's true, but while the themes might be about women needing their freedom, represented by their sealskins in this case, there are still many sightings of sealpeople and far too many stories to dismiss it outright,' ventures Cowrie.

'Hey, DK, that's true. Remember when I took you to see that John Sayles film, 'Roan Inish' at the Pacific Film Archives at University? About the little girl, Fiona, who was called back to find her brother who had been taken by the seals as a child. She found him floating in a little rounded boat, a coracle, that looked like a wooden clog, and eventually he was reunited with his family when they returned to the island they all left because the work had ended there. It was as if he and she were the symbolic link, the youth bringing the folk back home to their birthplaces to live and work instead of selling out to industrial interests and abandoning their heritage. I recall you being moved to tears if I remember correctly. You asked me if I felt the same being moved from our Chumash land and placed on a reservation and if I longed to return home again, like an ache inside the body.' Uretsete puts her hand on DK's knee.

DK's face lights up. 'Yeah, now I remember. Magic film. Isn't that why we wanted to visit Scotland and also explore Iona? It was that elemental feeling of belonging to something ancient, like, with more spiritual depth than just getting your degree and making money.'

'Right. And you said you'd love to be that little boy, Jamie, with the old stone house on the island, thatching the roof and fishing for food each day. You were right into it and into the sealfolk then, DK,' Uretsete reminds her.

DK blushes. 'Maybe so. But I sure am not afraid of some seal swimming up the Bay of Skaill to nab me. That's the least of my worries.'

'Then again, your folks did not just disappear without trace did they? I really felt for Shelley and I think she was very brave to tell us.'

'Maybe she wanted to do so before we heard it from others. Morrigan says the Orkney grapevine is faster than quicksilver. There's evidently one old codger who just sits in the Stromness pub and listens. The next day, it's all about town. So any time Morrigan wants to get word about, like when she is selling some cheap fish, she simply tells him and before she is back home people have started contacting her.' DK laughs at the thought.

'So what do you think about the sealfolk, Cowrie?' Uretsete asks. 'I mean after you told us all about Laukia-manuikahiki, the Hawai'ian turtle woman, I always associated her with you. You were both orphaned at birth and both were given sacred tokens to find your way back to your families later in life. So there must be some similar stories in your Maori and Hawai'ian traditions as in our Chumash one, right?'

Cowrie pauses a moment, then replies. 'Ae, Uretsete. Ka pae. You always manage to reach the heart of the matter. Maybe there's a spirit guide within each of us and maybe it assumes different forms according to our receptivity. But the selkie tradition is so strong here in these islands that I have begun to wonder about all this since coming. In the first week I was here, I picked up a book at Tam's bookstore in Stromness where some fella from the Isle of Harris in the Outer Hebrides had done decades of research into seal stories and made an interesting association between sightings of selkies and suggesting it could have been Eskimo or Inuit men in sea kayaks, which join the body at the waist, and who travelled this far down navigating by the stars. Few people believed him, but then again few believed that Pacific navigators could come from Hawai'i to Aotearoa in canoes and navigating by the stars until we did it again to prove the point. So he could have an interesting practical offering. Still, I like to think there are true selkies about too.'

'So what's this talk of selkies then?' Morrigan stands against the stone doorway, puffing on her pipe. 'You spinning yarns again Cowrie?'

DK jumps to Cowrie's defence and deflects the question back to Morrigan. 'D'you believe in the seal-folk, Morrigan?'

'Bloody nonsense, if you ask me,' asserts Morrigan. 'Tales told after too much whisky and in too much idle time with nothing better to do.' With that, she saunters off to collect her lobster pots and packs up the van for the night's fishing.

Cowrie, in silence, watches her through the window as she lugs the huge pots and wonders why she answered so brusquely and in denial of her previous statements. It's as if she is wanting to hide something. But what? And who is this man Kelpie? Did Morrigan have an affair with him behind the wife's back, or was he just a friend? Fancy him being Shelley's father.

'Ees it not rather strange how they have to keep discussing whether we exist or not, despite all the known evidence aboot selkies, when these Nofin humans will happily believe in aliens from space and even that they have been operated on by pale wee men with big almond eyes.' Sandy munches on the green sea lettuce as he talks.

'Soonds lyke yer average Edinburgh surgeon to me, Sandy,' Fiona replies, recalling her one journey down south from the island to have an operation when she was a Nofin. 'Mind you, I doot I'd have believed it meeself until yee dragged me from the beach and into the water that day.'

'I was a bit rough, but I feared yee'd not come voluntarily then. Yee were a wee beet uptight and suspicious, if yee don't mind me saying eet, Fe. T'was time for yee to change yer ways. Besides, yee'd often prayed to be released from the feudal lifestyle of yer family.'

'How d'yer know that, Sandy?' Fiona flicks some sand from her tail as she moves closer into the sea lettuce.

'The women of Skara Brae told me. They hold all the secrets of the island and release them when needed. That ees why they weer buried between the walls of Skara Brae, to be witnesses to our ways of living from the Stone Age onwards, and to find living creatures capable of acting on the information they've heard.'

'D'yer mean if they had not told you I was unhappy, yee'd never have known and come to rescue me?'

'I'd seen yee walking the shores of the Bay of Skaill in blustering winds and sometimes late at night or early in the morning, so I realised yee had things weighing on yer mind. But I did not realise your domestic situation was so bad until they contacted me.' Sandy spits out some shells that have attached themselves to a rocky ledge where he is searching for shrimps. 'Damned limpets, theyer soo hard on the stomach lining.'

'Why did they choose us to impart this knowledge to? Why not the longfins or gracefins?'

Sandy thinks a moment, flicking his tail in the face of a school of young mackerel, sending them fleeing on another seapath. 'I guess since we lived in the Bay and were close by, keeping an eye on things, and because we live on land and in the sea, then we were a perfect choice.'

Fiona pauses. 'Besides, there's been a long history of Nofin and seal exploits. I recall the butler discussing this with the maid when I was in the kitchen at Skaill. His coosin was out fishing one day. He never came home and two days later his upturned boat was found drifting off Finstown. Evidently, he'd been laying nets irresponsibly and many seals had been caught in them and died very slow and painful deaths. They tried to warn him by biting into his lines a few times but he simply strengthened them with steel wire. Finally, they obviously decided to get rid of him.' Fiona swims over to a more succulent piece of kelp.

'Steady on, Fiona. It wasn't thart hasty. From my recollection, they simply wanted to rock the boat a wee bit to scare him, let him know it was us seals protesting his actions. They swam up to the boat, nudging against the side gently. He started beatin' tharm with his oar, yelling oot that they were greedy bloody seals, eating fish meant for him. One youngfin was badly battered and blood flowed from his head. When the other seals saw this, they rocked the boat more, swimming under and around it, bumping the sides and bottom, in an attempt to stop him. The fisher got angry and cursed them, beating his oar over their heads. It was chaos, according to Scarpy, and it ended when he reached out too far, trying to hit the seals, and fell into the warter, upturning the boat. One of the seals tried to rescue him, nuzzled up to show him how to breathe, but he poked her in the eye and so they let him go, and watched, helpless, as he sank to the ocean floor. Scarpy says he'll never forget the man's eyes. They were cold, dark, terrified. Days later, they returned to the same spot and his eyes had been eaten by the shrimps. All that remained were eye sockets, and the mackerel were chewing into them with glee. None of the seals would touch the flesh. They knew it would be right tough and mean.' Sandy plunges his nose back into the sea lettuce, ripping off large chunks at a time.

Fiona stares into a rocky crevice searching for shrimps. She wonders what might have been her fate if she had not been so charmed by Sandy. Maybe she too would have been left on the ocean floor, with shrimps aiming for her eye sockets before her body had begun to decompose. She shudders at the thought, the movement of her fins alerting the shrimps to their intended fate, and they swing around and head back into the heart of their sandstone cave.

[16]

'Hey, look at this!' Uresete points to a column in the *Orcadian* and reads. 'Call for weekend workshops. Literature, art, meditation, gardening, archeology, Orkney walks. You devise a course and we'll help you organise it. Please apply to Dotty Network at PO Box 193, Stromness, or email Dotty@Stromness.demon.co.uk and check out our web site below.' Let's organise a storytelling workshop, and combine local stories with our own performances in a festival for the public later.'

'Right on! That's why we came in the first place,' adds DK. 'Well, part of the reason.' She glances at Uretsete, winking.

Morrigan glances up from her work. 'Bloody wankers, those academics. Dotty couldn't organise a piss up in a brewery.'

'Morrigan. Watch your language,' admonishes Camilla, ironing Morrigan's fishing jumper.

'Beats the hell out of me why you are doing that, woman,' Morrigan says. 'The bloody sweater will be full of fish guts and crab claws within twelve hours and buggered if they care whether it's ironed or not.'

'Well, I do, Morrigan. And you should have more pride in your appearance. You're a very handsome woman when you clean yourself up.'

Morrigan laughs and winks at DK. 'She'll be wanting to marry me soon.' She grimaces and returns to her paper. Camilla irons on, taking no notice of Morrigan's bit of lip. She's used to it at home and somehow, despite the roughness of this place, she is getting to like its honesty. And Morrigan surely needs a steady woman to look after her. She has a heart of gold, even if she lacks a few refinements, admits Camilla, as she works her way carefully around the buttons, making sure she does not miss any creases.

'I think the workshops are a grand idea.' Sasha glances from her sketch pad, which is covered in kayaks and seals and designs of sealskin boats where the paddlers inside look like humans with seal bodies, entering into the water from an iceberg. Cowrie looks at the drawings over her shoulder and admits that early Inuit paddlers in sealskin boats could easily have appeared to be selkies, especially as they entered the water or when they skimmed up the beach to peel off their spray skirts, leaving the sealskin kayak behind. To early islanders, who had not seen kayaks before, it may look like they are one creature shedding its skin. Then again, the theory does not explain all the other sightings and stories of selkie women that had nothing to do with the Inuit kayakers, she ponders.

'Me too,' replies Cowrie. 'I'd enjoy listening to more stories from these islands, other than those I've heard and gleaned from a few past Orcadian newspapers. And I'd like to share some Pacific stories with Orcadians. Most of their knowledge of Aotearoa is South Island, New Zealand, where their relatives live in the colder climes of Christchurch or Dunedin, and that's very much white folks' territory other than a few Kai Tahu descendants. I reckon they'd enjoy some Maori and Pacific Island myths and talkstory. I mean, we are all fishers and island people with much in common. From what I see here, it's very like the wild West Coast of the South Island, Hokitika to Westport. Similar climate, similar culture, similar humour and a strange mixture of anti-bureaucratic left-wing union politics with a dash of right-wing church parish morality. Throw in a few beautiful, rugged wind-swept beaches and a wild passion for whitebait that here might be lobster, and you're pretty much at home.'

This raises a chuckle from Morrigan. 'Reckon you've got us figured out, eh, Cowrie? You're pretty accurate on most counts, but you forgot the whisky.'

'So I did! There's more than one whitebaiter with a whisky tale or two. A Kai Tahu Maori and Kirkwall Orcadian writer, Keri Hulme, it is said, was working on her second large novel, *Bait*. The one after *The Bone People*, that scooped the Booker award and caused some controversy, mainly among jealous writers who felt they should have won it. Anyway, she signed up with the publishers for the sequel, *Bait*, but still wanted time to work on it. Evidently they kept sending faxes asking when it was coming, so eventually she dried a small whitebait, about an inch long, placed it in cotton wool inside a matchbox, and sent it off to them. She then faxed saying, '*Bait* is on its way at last. Arohanui — Keri.' Luckily they thought it was funny and gave her some space to finish writing the text. Well, I reckon she'd had a dram or two of Highland Park to pull off a feat like that, though I may be wrong. She has a bloody good sense of humour sober too!' Cowrie laughs at the memory of the story and the others love it too.

'Now that's the kind of woman I'd like to hang about with.' Morrigan chuckles at the idea of pulling off such a stunt.

'Here's a start, Morrigan.' Cowrie extracts her battered, well-read copy of *The Bone People* from her backpack. 'Check this out and then tell me what you think.' Morrigan takes the book and fingers the artwork on the cover, admiring it.

'That's Keri's work too. She was an artist exhibiting at the Women's Gallery in Wellington before she was well known as a writer.' Cowrie points to the acknowledgments in the book.

Morrigan is impressed. She opens the book at the preface and reads aloud: 'They were nothing more than people, by themselves. Even paired, any pairing, they would have been nothing more than people by themselves. But all together, they have become the heart and muscles and mind of something perilous and new, something strange and growing and great. Together, all together, they are the instruments of change.'

'Wow,' says DK. 'That's awesome. That pretty well sums up why we exist, I reckon.' The others agree. 'Isn't that the book you set us to read at UC, Cowrie? Where the young boy gets washed up on the beach and it turns out . . .'

'Yeah, DK, so don't wreck the story for Morrigan,' Uretsete injects.

'Ooops, sorry Morrigan'.

But Morrigan is too engrossed in the writing to notice. She wanders outside to her favourite reading place under the sycamore tree, one of the few which has withstood the Orkney storms, and slides her back down the tree until she reaches the sandstone rock ledge below, never taking her eyes off the page. Cowrie watches from the window. 'Well that's Morrigan taken care of for the day.'

'Didn't *The Bone People* come out in Germany as *Unter dem Tagmond* a few years ago?' asks Monique, still examining her photos of Skara Brae.

'I think so,' replies Cowrie. 'What does it mean in German?'

'Hard to translate literally. It's something like "under the day moon". An unusual and captivating title.'

'Now I remember some fuss regarding the title reported in the media,' Cowrie puts in. 'As I recall there was some debate over whether a German audience would take to a title like "*The Bone People*", given their nervousness about bone imagery post-holocaust.'

'That wouldn't be surprising,' admits Monique. 'It wasn't only the Jews and gays who were hunted down and taken to the death camps. Heaps of African-Germans were gassed to death and others were sterilised in a desperate attempt to prevent more of us being born. It was all-out ethnic cleansing. But few of our parents spoke out against it. They were terrified after that and tried to remain as inconspicuous as possible.'

'How come we've not heard about it in the African-American community then?' asks DK.

'Different issues. Africans living in the States have their own battles to fight. But in Germany, our communities are fewer and more closeted. It has only been more recently, and since Katharina Oguntoye's film about Black Survivors of the Holocaust, that more of us have spoken out. My father was sterilised after he had me and it devastated him. My mother said he was never the same again. He'd at least had one child. Many younger men were sterilised as teenagers and never had the chance to have families. Family and kinship is vital to our culture and the Nazis knew this. They figured if they sterilised the men, their spirits as well as their bodies would be affected. It worked. But now, more are speaking out and others are learning the courage we have together. Kosovo showed us it can happen all over again with the so-called ethnic cleansing of Albanians.'

'True enough,' adds Uretsete. 'I'm all for speaking out. The silence and patience of my own Chumash tribe never did us any good. And I wish the media would stop calling the brutal extermination of races "ethnic cleansing". It is violent racism, and all forms of racism have the potential to lead to this. So when they call us 'politically correct', we need to answer that Hitler and Milosovich and Sadam Hussein were allowed to flourish because people were lax and not politically correct or astute or whatever word you like. Once your people or family are exterminated, sterilised, tortured, then you can never make light of such terms again.'

'Language is power, and how we use it reveals the power structures,' Cowrie offers. 'So what can we do? I believe that education is a part of the answer and storytelling is an entertaining way people can learn about other cultures without being as threatened as they might at a political rally or similar.' She finishes the dishes with a clang against the saucepan, as if to emphasise her point.

'Yes. It puts one in a more relaxed state.' Camilla stops her ironing to join in. 'Years ago, I could never have imagined sharing space with such radical activists and storytellers as you. But despite my inherited conservatism, I agree with you on the power of education, though we approach it differently. I'm all for us organising a workshop and I think we should listen to Morrigan's advice on the best approach to involve local Orcadians.'

'I agree,' says Sasha. 'It's crucial we have local support for this. I reckon we should run it like a workshop, hearing the local stories first, and just include our work in the evening performance sessions, so that we do not take over their event. That way, the different approaches will come across and we just facilitate the groups. It's more a matter of careful listening skills all round.'

'Wunderbar!' claps Monique. So how will we organise the sessions and who wants to take what?' She gets out a sheet of paper and begins taking notes as they gather around and plan the workshop, intending to run it by Morrigan later to see what she thinks.

Under the sycamore tree, Morrigan is captivated by the crustaceans in the rock pools of Aotearoa, by the waves pounding the west coast beaches, the call of the wild, the strange presence of the mute child and the aikido-happy guitar playing, whitebait-addicted Kerewin. She wonders what it would be like to be Orcadian and Maori at once, whether the two tribal links are warring within or similar at heart. Maybe it's like being part human and part seal. But which part is which? She chuckles at the thought and burrows her nose back into the book.

[17]

The sheep lie in the fields munching their cud. It is three in the morning, still light and the sun is beginning to rise. Over the hill come five women warriors, armed with sketch books, cameras and binoculars. The leader of the troupe is playing a bone flute and its haunting sounds shimmer out over the valley, waking the drowsing cows and black-faced sheep and peedie Shetland horses. The music enters into the twenty-seven frozen shapes standing still in a circle. As the sun rises over the Loch of Harray it causes long shadows to emanate from the towering stone as the women walk silently around the perimeter of the ancient, sacred Ring of Brodgar.

When they have completed the circle, a vibrating cry issues from a nearby burial mound, followed by a soul-piercing karanga, calling in the ancestors to the ring and welcoming the manuhiri. It sends a shuddering excitement up the spine of the women. Cowrie emerges from the other side of the mound and walks toward the women, placing her hei matau on the sacred ground as a welcome. Sasha recognises this is a greeting and bends to pick it up, accept the challenge, and Cowrie then places the bone fish-hook carving around her neck. Uretsete burns some sweetgrass she has brought with her and Sasha fingers her flute and is answered by a lone pied oystercatcher perched atop one of the stones.

The sun reflects a silver band across the loch and the stone shapes vibrate with energy. Each one has its own sense of presence, its own particular shape and moss designs and runic inscriptions from the rain and wind. Cowrie notes this, adding, '. . . but together, all together, they are the instruments of change,' quoting her favourite book, and thinking about the vast worldy changes witnessed by the silent vigil of the Ring and the Standing Stones of Stenness nearby.

'Awesome. There really is a sacredness here missing from the touristicised Stonehenge and many other sites. Maybe it's the perfect circle of the ring, or the awe of standing under stones nearly triple your height, or maybe it's being on a thin strip of land between two lochs and knowing you can face the sunrise or the sunset over water, but this place surely is holy,' utters Uretsete, clearly moved by being here. Even Camilla is touched, and the group has not seen her like this before. Cowrie notices a softness and vulnerability in her eyes which she normally keeps well guarded.

'How and why did they build such vast monuments?' asks DK.

'If we could answer that, DK, we'd be in great demand by now. I've read archeological reports and listened to local theories since arriving here, and all offer a wide range of ideas. One of the most interesting is a mathematician, Alexander Thom, who reckoned that these stone circles were based on extremely complex geometry. If he's correct, then these neolithic Stone-age people understood the triangle about 2500 years before its theory was devised by Pythagoras.'

'How ridiculous,' asserts Camilla. 'As if that is possible.'

'Why not?' answers Uretsete. 'My ancestors practised sustainable existence, living in tune with nature, long before modern ecologists reinvented the idea and claimed it for themselves. Why do we always have to assume the modern outclasses the ancient?'

Cowrie supports her. 'It's true, Camilla. You can't

argue with that. Most indigenous tribes lived a far more balanced ecology working with the sea and land rather than farming it to extinction, and only now are we seeing the wisdom of those ways again.'

'That's too simplistic. It could be that these stones were simply ceremonial sites or for some kind of decoration, like we build statues to celebrate this or that king, queen or explorer.'

'Now who's being simplistic,' answers Sasha. 'Look at these stones and the deep ditch around them. They would have taken years to construct even with a large workforce. Imagine the skill in digging the stones from the ditches and then moving them on pulleys or similar and raising them in a perfect circle. Stones that are three times our heights. They must have cut holes at the base and rammed rocks in to hold them up. I can't imagine that they would have invested so much human energy just for decoration.'

'There's evidence from pottery and bones found in excavations at the nearby Stones of Stenness, see, just down there, that both they and the Ring were places of important ceremonial occasions, so maybe you are both right,' suggests Cowrie, wanting to avoid a confrontation at this sacred site. 'Radio carbon analysis of bones and charcoal from the site shows they were constructed about 3000 BCE and that the charcoal in the centre of the stones meant fires were held there. Pottery they call Grooved Ware links the site to similar shards found at Skara Brae and Barnhouse, showing that people must have come from all over Orkney to celebrate here.'

Camilla nods her head. 'That's true. Morrigan told me that human burials and animal sacrifice, feasting, dedication ceremonies and spiritual practices can all be deducted from the archeological finds.'

'And I believe Alexander Thom showed the various stones connected to lunar alignments and he stated the observatory was used to track the movements of the moon several thousand years BCE. I like that idea'. Cowrie looks up to the sky and imagines being here at midnight, tracking the moon just as her ancestors navigated by stars to find their way across the Pacific to Aotearoa in canoes.

'Then maybe the Ring is a huge sacred communal place, like an ampitheatre or arena, where some star-gazed and others laughed and sang and played music and told stories around the fire,' suggests Uretsete, getting excited about the possibilities of this.

'Could be. Wouldn't it be awesome if we could get permission to hold a workshop performance out here? Maybe using the Ring as a backdrop rather than performing in it, since the heather ring within the circle should not be destroyed.' DK's eyes light up at the suggestion. 'Let's check it out.' The others agree it would be fantastic.

'So, if the pottery found here is the same as at Skara Brae, then it is likely that the same people who lived in Skara Brae constructed and then visited this site, right?' asks Monique.

'Sounds like it. So?'

'When I went to Skara Brae to take photographs, the guide told us that many people believed, from the evidence of domestic life there and the lack of anything showing a male presence, that it could have been a community of women living together. Furthermore, archeological evidence shows it was an egalitarian society without rigid hierarchies. So, if the women built and lived in Skara Brae, then maybe they designed or built the Ring of Brodgar too?'

'I'd go for that. It has an amazingly female energy compared to a place like Stonehenge,' adds Uretsete.

'Don't be ridiculous,' interjects Camilla. 'As if women would be strong enough to construct and raise huge stones like these.' She scoffs at the idea that this could be even suggested.

'Not so fast, Camilla. Have you seen the artist's sketches of the Skara Brae women's community in Legendary Britain based on the archeological evidence? It shows Inuit women, large and strong, with painted bodies and bearing hand-made tools, one carrying a huge sack of Orkney oysters home. It depicted them being totally self-sufficient hunter-gatherers, long before the blokes imported farming and taming of the land rituals. They had teepee-like structures above the land as well as the domestic houses beneath the land. It blew my mind to see this painting.'

'But surely an artist's impression is simply that — an impression?' argues Camilla.

'Yes, but based on archeological data. That's all we can do to reconstruct accurately what may have been. I'm not saying it had to be this way, but it is interesting to keep an open mind and consider all the possibilities. Like with our storytelling. Our talkstory reflects other ways of interpreting existence and is handed down and added to as society grows and progresses.' Cowrie sees the hurt look in Camilla's eyes. 'Hey, it's just a suggestion Camilla. It's not a matter of who is right or wrong but expanding our perceptions to include all possibilities.'

'I must admit, I like the idea of a women's community here and at Skara Brae,' admits Camilla, 'as unlikely as I think it is.'

'One archeologist, Dr Anna Ritchie, who excavated neolithic sites and wrote extensively about Orkney, did a close study of the development of the pottery from Unstan Ware to Grooved Ware and concluded that it could have marked the changes from a matriarchal society to a patriarchal one, from the evidence gathered.' Cowrie is keen to encourage Camilla's attempt to remain open.

Quark! Quark! The oystercatcher deems the women have by now moved too close to her nest, hidden in rocks near the perimeter ditch, and she swoops down in front of them, issuing sharp cries of protest.

'Time we moved away and left her in peace, I reckon,' suggests Sasha, noting her plea.

They sit in silence on the mound facing the ring, meditating the ideas for some time as the sun edges slowly around the stones. They record their impressions in sketches, notes, photographs and music, with Sasha composing a new flute melody where the leitmotif returns again and again, circling the song, just like the stones.

After some time, they have a picnic brunch they have brought, enjoying the thought of ancient women feasting around this site just as they do now, and lay out oatcakes and cheese, tomatoes and rocket, melon and mangoes. Cowrie offers a karakia to bless the food and they savour the tastes, and wash it down with Orcadian mineral water which Morrigan collects from a site once used by all but later boarded up by companies fearing competition. She believes it is from the land and should be shared with everyone. It is a fitting wine for the occasion.

After a luscious feast, many more stories and some bone flute music on Cowrie's koauau, weaving melodies with Sasha's wooden flute, they head off into the hills on the return journey to the Bay of Skaill. The sun shines directly down on the stones, dwarfing their shadows and indicating it is as near noon today as it may have been near noon at this site five thousand years ago. Sasha's flute warns the sheep, horses and birds as they draw near and allows them a peaceful walk home. The curlews in the fields call in answer with their haunting cries, echoing her song.

[18]

'Hamnavoe, the bay of Stromness, is a fine deep anchorage sheltered from everything but a south-easterly gale,' DK reads from the Stromness Heritage Guide. They make their way along the main street, flanked on both sides by ancient stone dwellings packed together like sardines and sprouting up three stories in height. The narrow curving street, more a lane by modern standards, follows the shore line and every few feet you can glance down narrow alleys to see brightly coloured fishing boats bobbing up and down on the water. The waterfront, with its stone piers and slipways, is said to resemble a Norwegian fishing village.

'So this is the town of George Mackay Brown's poetry,' hums Sasha. 'It really lives up to the imagery and atmosphere.' Most of the shops are at street level, housed in domestic buildings, keeping the feel of an old village rather than modern spaces designed purely for commerce. Buildings are sculpted from slate and sandstone from grey to ochre, and flagstones and cobblestones in various earthy colours form the street surface.

'What road are we on?' asks Uretsete, looking for a signpost.

'We came in on John Street, but it looks from this map like the same main street follows the shoreline right through the town, changes about here into Victoria Street, with the post office and chippy and bakery, and further down into Graham Place, then Dundas and Alfred Streets.'

'Isn't Graham Place where they knocked down some old buildings to allow cars to fit through? I read it somewhere in a brochure on the 'St Ola',' remarks Cowrie.

'Yes,' replies Uretsete. 'A damned pity too,' as she steps aside to let a yuppy Range-Rover edge past. 'Should be for pedestrians only, not pollution pushers.' They laugh at her terminology, but agree the town would be much more attractive without vehicles and especially since the central shopping area is easily walkable.

'Forty-two Dundas Street,' reads DK from the brochure, 'was the home of Eliza Fraser whose shipwreck and experiences in Queensland, Australia, in 1835 are the subject of several books and a film.'

'Now that's your territory, Cowrie,' smiles Sasha, 'so spill the beans, old girl.'

'Queensland sure ain't my territory, gorgeous,' she grins back. 'Nor yours, coz it's the home of racist politicians and policies. It's right-wing redneck territory, but fortunately, that's also what breeds pirates like Lizzie and cowgirls and dykes and all sorts of other exceptions to the mainstream.'

'But isn't there a local woman pirate from Stromness? She lived somewhere up from the Back Road, according to Morrigan, just under Brinkies Brae in the late eighteenth and early nineteenth centuries,' comments Camilla. 'Her real name was Bessie Millie but Sir Walter Scott called her Norny of the Fitful Head in his novel *The Pirate*. It's said she sold fair winds to sailors.'

'I read about that too. And for a fair price, enterprising soul that she was,' adds Cowrie.

They walk the length and breadth of the township, noting places of interest and learning about the colourful history of Stromness. Sasha is fascinated to discover that Rae's Close is named after Dr John Rae, an Orcadian Arctic explorer for the Hudson's Bay Company who completed the mapping of Northern Canada. She'd heard about him but had no idea he was Orcadian. She tells them about a group of Inuit school children who were being retaught the special Inuit ways of playing the fiddle, which had been taken to her land originally by Orcadians. That first interested her in visiting Orkney one day, along with the wild sea stories that were told about Orkney and the early whaling days.

Following the harbour along the Ness Road, they see the former Sule Skerry Shore Station, built in 1892 to house the families of the lighthouse keepers living on Sule Skerry. They learn that the harbour side of Point Ness was let to herring curers, then walk on back to the fish shop to sample some of the delicious Stromness herring marinated in a range of sauces: with dill, sherry, juniper and even aged whisky.

'When was Stromness first settled?' Cowrie asks the old man leaning against the door of the Stromness Fish Shop as if he is a part of the stonework.

'If yee go by The Orkneyinga Saga, written in the twelfth century, Earl Harald Maddadson fled from his cousin Erland and hid in the Castle of Cairston in September 1152,' he relates, as if it were yesterday. 'But the first recorded settlement was up there.' He points to the east, 'and they talk of a hoose at Garston on the Cairston Shore in 1492. But the date us fishermen like to remember is 1590 when the inn was built in Hamnavoe which took in sailors from visiting ships. Aye, thems were thee daiys.' He takes a draft on his pipe, and looks down the main road nostalgically, as if he could summon up the sailors and tall ships and smell of the whisky before his eyes now, and he sighs.

'So how did this port get the name Hamnavoe?'

The old fisherman shifts from one yellow boot to the

other and adjusts his stance against the wall, taking another big suck on his pipe. 'From the invading Vikings, lass. They came here in their longboats and thar's many an Orcadian descended from them Vikings. Aye, and many more who dinna ken admit it.' He pulls the pipe from his mouth, pokes his finger into it, pressing down the remaining tobacco, and proceeds to refill it from a rusted tin with a picture of a lighthouse on the lid which he keeps in his trouser pocket.

Cowrie reaches deep into her jacket and takes out a bone and paua fish-hook, fashioned after the early Maori ones, and shows it to him. 'Ever seen a fish-hook like this?' She places it in his hand. He strokes his yellowing grey beard and mumbles some words she cannot make out. Then he turns to her. 'Aye, lassie. Somethin akin to this, at Skara Brae. Tools shaped from bone, arrowheads, fish hooks, but nothin quite like this.' He turns it over to see how the paua shell has been attached with twine to the carved bone hook. 'And this be abalone?' he asks, polishing it with his finger then holding it up to the light. 'All the colours of the rainbow. Must come from the promised land.'

Cowrie grins. 'Ae, paua from Aotearoa, land of the awakening dawn.' She curves his fingers around the carved bone and tells him to keep it. His eyes light up and he presses her hand. 'Thank yee, lassie. The rainbow shell will brighten me up on days when the sou-easters bluster into Hamnavoe and I leave me old haunts and skuttle into the Ferry Inn for a wee dram. Maybe I'll see yer there some day?'

'For sure.' Cowrie smiles, then hurries to join the others, now half-way down an alley to the waterfront. There they lean over the rails watching the dories and old fishing vessels moving in and out the harbour and fishermen washing down the decks or carrying large sacks of fish up the wharf. Their bright yellow rubber boots distinguish the fishers and sailors from the wharf officials and ferryloopers piling off the 'St Ola'.

They take turns with the binoculars, noting with glee the names of boats: 'Morning Dawn', 'Dyke's End', 'Arctic Explorer', 'Vanishing Tides', 'Suzie Q', 'Quoyloo', 'Kelpie', 'Fulmar', 'Puffin' and 'No Puffin', no doubt owned by non-smokers — a rare breed on the islands, '10345–Bay of Skaill', 'Selkie Too', 'Hoy Ho'. Cowrie asks Sasha for the binoculars. She turns back in the direction Sasha had been looking and, sure enough, there is Morrigan on the deck of the 'Selkie Too' bending over a large sack. Three men are looking down from the wharf. One by one they jump into the boat and help her lift the bundle, which looks like a drowned body, onto a flat trailer on the wharf. 'Hey, Camilla. Did Morrigan come home from fishing last night?' she asks.

'Not before I left. She usually comes in early, has oatmeal porridge to warm up, then slumps into her bed. Why?'

'Nothing, just wondered,' returns Cowrie, zooming in on the bundle the men have lifted up from the boat. The body stirs slightly, or else has been bumped by their movement. She holds the binoculars steady and zooms in again. It is a seal. The creature lifts its head from the net a moment, opens its eyes wide, then lies down again, as if too exhausted to move. But not before Cowrie has seen the eyes close up. There's something about them, something familiar. Somewhere she's seen these eyes before.

[19]

Morrigan stays away the next three days and nights and when she returns is morose and withdrawn. She ignores them all, even Camilla. Camilla senses something very upsetting has happened but all her hints to share the pain reach deaf ears. Morrigan retreats into her book and eats little, coming into the kitchen to prepare food and taking it back to her room. Camilla visits the others in Cowrie and Sasha's cottage and they work on refining a proposal for the storytelling workshops.

'If only she would open out to me,' moans Camilla. 'Unburden herself. Sometimes I think she carries around dark secrets in her soul and she needs to open herself to God to reach a state of peace.'

'Maybe so, Camilla, but it could simply be a bad fishing week from what I have seen of Morrigan's mood swings,' suggests Monique. 'God never did much for my grievances. In fact, he was used to support racism and homophobia in many cases. I don't have a lot of time for the old bearded man in the skies myself.'

'That's simply not true. He was never bigoted. It is just some churches and people who take the bible very literally who use the texts in that way to support their own bigotry in ignorance rather than hatred,' replies Camilla.

'It's pretty hard to distinguish that kind of ignorance from hatred when your own people are cast aside for the colour of their skin or their belief systems,' replies Monique.

Cowrie senses a pointless feud about to erupt, with each side arguing and neither listening, and steps in by asking Camilla what, specifically, she thinks is wrong with Morrigan. Camilla gives this some thought and replies that it is certainly something to do with the spirit that is eating at her rather than money or material concerns. Monique is about to challenge her and ask what presumption she is using to judge such a situation but Cowrie's frown warns her off and she returns to her cataloguing of the Skara Brae photographs. It is clear to her that Cowrie is on some line of inquiry for some purpose and, besides, Camilla is a right-wing fundamentalist, as far as Monique is concerned, and thus not worth arguing with really. Cowrie persists. 'But you have been quite close to her over these past few weeks. What do you think could be worrying her spiritually so much?' 'I don't know, Cowrie. I'm not her confessor,' Camilla replies, abruptly, clearly not happy that the answer has eluded her also.

'Well, she has seemed to give different versions of events at times, according to the occasion, and I find that usually means a covering up for someone or something,' Cowrie suggests tentatively.

'Maybe so,' Camilla admits, recalling those early few days with Morrigan. 'But deep down I believe she is a woman of integrity, even though she seems to waver from time to time. You should be more forgiving, Cowrie. Look at how hard she works, fishing every night and seldom taking time off.'

'True,' says Cowrie, also remembering the times Morrigan was in the fields keeping watch on the cottage and not out fishing in the first few days after they arrived, and her odd appearance at the pub or in other places when fishing has been the cover. Then what about the chest she found in the shed, which has since disappeared, and the strange case of the dying seal in her net yesterday at Stromness?

83

When they had asked her if she had come back to Finstown, she replied yes. But when pushed, and after she realised they had seen her in Stromness with a dying seal in her net, she admitted that one had got caught by mistake in some fisherman's net. Not hers, she added quickly, since she is a crab and lobster fisher, requiring creels not nets. She'd rescued it on realising it was dying and brought it in to be taken to the Seal Rescue Centre for help. Later, Cowrie called the SRC to ask how it was and they said nobody had bought in a wounded seal for three weeks and they hoped it would stay that way. 'If any are found,' the woman had added, 'we always get to know about it.' 'Island Seal-line,' she volunteered, with a chuckle.

Uretsete suggests they focus on the workshops again if they hope to get out that afternoon, so they discuss various ways of facilitating such workshops to get the most from the participants. Again the idea of getting permission to hold a celebration where the workshop participants get to share their stories around a fire on a site near the Ring of Brodgar is discussed. Maybe a few musicians could help turn it into a ceilidh. Camilla will check with Morrigan about who owns the nearest land and, failing that, will approach the Orkney Islands Council and the Scottish Heritage Trust.

'What happens if none of them are open to it?' asks DK. 'Do we just invade the land like the groups at Stonehenge each solstice?'

'No. It is sacred land and we need to convince the people in charge that we intend to use it sacredly, much in line with how it was used ceremonially in the neolithic period,' Uretsete says. 'How can they object to that?'

'Oh, they can indeed,' replies Cowrie, telling them of the peaceful occupation of Maori land at Bastion Point,

Auckland, and how, after 501 days of occupation, more police and army were brought in than occupiers, and they literally dragged men, women, elders and children from their own land.

'So what happened after that?' asks Monique.

'The state had used the land behind for housing and wanted more, since it was prime real estate. After that, there was so much support for the Maori occupation that they were forced to give the land back, so everyone could enjoy it.'

'I recall you telling us about that on Great Turtle Island,' adds Uretsete, 'and it was inspiring to many Navajo and Hopi fighting to retain Big Mountain, Arizona at the time.'

'Ae. The only hope for our survival is to work together and inspire each other,' replies Cowrie. 'Besides, it's much more fun than suffering in silence.'

'Try telling Morrigan,' replies Camilla, sighing.

'Don't worry, Camilla. She'll come right. She's bound to have her reasons,' Sasha offers. 'Just let her be.'

'Just let who be?' Morrigan asks, suddenly appearing in the doorway. 'You gossiping about me again, then?' She looks accusingly at Cowrie, then Camilla.

'No,' replies Camilla truthfully, 'we're simply concerned.'

'Well, get unconcerned then. There's nothing wrong. Now do you want me to look over those workshop plans or not?' Morrigan sits down next to DK and surveys the written ideas. 'Not bad,' she admits, 'for a bunch of ferryloopers, that is.' She grins. 'But you'll need to do more to get locals talking about their family stories. I think you should add a workshop here starting with something very simple, like telling a story about a piece of jewellery or a stone or a hunk of furniture. You'll be amazed at what emerges, then build on the stories from there. They have a productive session with Morrigan contributing and Cowrie wonders again if she has simply been too suspicious of Morrigan. She's a good sort really and there is usually a credible explanation for her inconsistencies. Besides, we all have them. She resolves to lay off and concentrate on enjoying the company of the women, especially Sasha, whom she has been very close to since their day at the Brough of Birsay.

Morrigan stretches her long legs and yawns. 'That's a damned site harder than a night's fishing,' she claims. 'What say we all pile into the van and I take you over to the cliffs at Yesnaby to see if we can find any wild Orcadian primroses.'

'Wonderful,' replies Camilla, delighted that Morrigan is cheerful again. '*Primula Scotica*. That's the wild-flowers, correct?'

'Those doon south pinch all our best wildflowers and name them after the Scots,' Morrigan answers.

'Then how come your most famous whisky is called Highland Park, after the Scottish Highlands?' asks DK, tempting Morrigan to a rebuttal.

'It was originally Hoy-land and some of the clan misunderstood, no doubt,' mumbles Morrigan, suppressing a grin.

They climb into the van and Morrigan drives them out on narrow farm roads to Yesnaby, pointing to sites of interest on the way. They park right at the cliff edge and walk over the hills, finding only a small patch of the wildflowers, then return to the high rock ledges towering out over the water. Cowrie and Sasha clamber to the very edge and perch themselves on a flat rock, bracing their feet against the wind on another ledge, with the others finding their own special places to watch the sunset. To their left is a large geo or chasm where the sea invades the rock and swirls inland to crash up against the rocky interior and be pushed back out like a wave in reverse, in turn smashing into the next incoming wave and causing water to spout up as if from huge whales lying beneath the sea. One of the far cliffs has a hole in it where waves crash through. Fulmars and guillemots glide below them, high up on the wind, struggling to make it back to their nests without being smashed into the rocks. The wind rips into the cliffs and flings pieces of heather and grass from the tufts in the rocks where they eek out a precarious existence. Sasha turns to Cowrie. 'Wanna kiss, sweetheart?'

'Too shy here, my little arctic tern. Wait until we are home.'

'Tender Turtle, too soft for the cliff edge of Yesnaby.' She nudges Cowrie warmly and they cuddle together in their oilskins to warm themselves against the wild westerly battering into the cliff face. From behind, they look like two seals perched on their rocks, ready to slide into the sea. Below them, Camilla trembles as Morrigan strides out to the edge of the cliff and peers over, as if looking for something in the surf. She stands there some time and for a chilling moment, when the wind surges in, Cowrie has the sensation that Morrigan is going to jump off. She stretches to her full height, leans out over the cliff and wavers a moment. Camilla calls her back. Morrigan leans further forward then a huge wave crashes up over her and forces her back to the inner part of the ledge where Camilla grabs her.

Sasha and Cowrie look at each other in disbelief, thinking the same unutterable thought. Was Morrigan really about to top herself, in front of them all, after she'd seemed so much cheerier this afternoon? Yesnaby is famous for its dramatic suicides. Once a person has launched off the cliff, even if they survived after hitting the sea, their bodies would be frozen in minutes, or smashed alive against the rocky crags below. But why on earth would she even contemplate such a move? What could drive her to this desperation, wonders Cowrie, silently.

They watch the sunset with no further dramas, and drive back in silence, each within her own space, DK and Uretsete contemplating the sunset, having not seen the drama, Camilla worrying about Morrigan, Sasha and Cowrie internally debating if what they saw really was what they thought, and Morrigan wondering why she had not had the courage to stay at the edge of the cliff when the wave surfed over her.

By the time they return home, Morrigan is surly again and suggests they catch the boat to Hoy the next day since there is an excellent walk around the island to see the tall 450-foot rock named the Man of Hoy at the other side. Besides, she admits, she's not going fishing tonight and would like a day of peace alone at the cottage if they don't mind. Of course, they agree to go, but Camilla lies in bed hoping she will not do anything silly and Cowrie also wonders if she should be left alone after this evening's drama. Sasha is sure Morrigan can look after herself and holds Cowrie in her arms, crooning into her ear. 'Just remember that awesome sunset, Turtle, and let go of the clouds. The way that huge ball of fire sank into the sea, sending up orange and fiery light onto the bellies of the clouds above until they gleamed red. Recall those small billowy dragons spouting smoke from cream clouds turning to pink as they passed by, and the seal in the water which poked her head up and watched, as if looking at the humans looking at the sunset.'

'What seal?' asks Cowrie. 'I didn't see any seal.'

'It was right below Morrigan when she hung out over the cliff edge. I thought she was trying to get a better look at it, actually, then teetered a bit before the wave crashed in.'

'I never saw that. You have sharp sight, Sasha,' Cowrie replies.

'Dolphin radar,' Sasha says, smiling. Cowrie kisses her on the cheek, cuddling into her, happy to be here. Sasha noses her way into Cowrie's back, curling around her, holding her Turtle and humming softly into her shell.

[20]

'Look, dolphins, port-side,' yells Sasha into the wind as they pass close to the island of Cava. They rush to the left side of the roll-on, roll-off ferry from Houton to Hoy, to see seven dolphins leaping from the water and heading toward their bow. Once they have caught up with the speed of the boat, they split into two groups, four one side of the bow and three the other and take turns in leaping as close as possible to the boat without ever getting hurt, while keeping perfect time with the ferry. They stay, exuberantly slicing the waters and playing with the boat as if she were another creature, until they near the island of Flotta. Then, as if knowing they are nearing a potential danger zone, they deftly leave the bow, as effortlessly as they arrived, and head off into the open sea.

The massive structure of the Flotta Oil Terminal rises up from the island like a hideous growth. Morrigan explained to them earlier that it was considered a wonderful supplier of jobs to islands which have lost so much of their workforce to mainland Scotland, so was generally treated as a positive influence. But Cowrie and Sasha both argued that it was a huge risk to islands so dependant on tourism for survival as well as their fishing industry. The cost of a small oil spill, let alone a massive one, could nearly wipe out the island economy and it would be too late for regrets once it had happened.

Now, they vigorously debate the pros and cons, with Sasha detailing the vast and hideous effects of the Exxon Valdez oil spill off the Alaskan Coast. She had been there visiting her Uncle Ben, who was involved in the salmon fishing industry, and the small business he ran with five other fishers was destroyed after the spill. All the men had to go on the unemployment benefit and some helped in the clean up, including Ben. For two weeks she went with him, each day picking up more dead seabirds and loading them onto trucks to be buried. Those still alive were carefully washed down and held at bird rescue centres, set up along the coastline, and returned to the water as soon as it was safe enough. But several ended up caught in the oil again when the winds and tides changed. Sometimes it seemed as if the slick had a life of its own and was following them, closing in on them as soon as they had cleared another stretch of coastline.

'It was impossible to clean up. We simply did the best possible, but the oil seeped past the rocks and deep into the sands, killing shellfish and any vegetation near the shores, as well as seabirds and fish and seals and dolphins. Oil-soaked whales were found with their spouts blocked by the substance and they drifted towards the shores to be stranded in a black mass of treacle thick scum floating on the surface.'

'But I thought they managed to contain the oil slick eventually and it was all cleaned up with rigorous attention to detail,' comments Camilla, wrapping her scarf around her neck against the cold south-easterly.

'That's what Exxon would have you believe. They swung into action with their spin-doctors and PR consultants and paid scientists huge sums to say the right things, but I can tell you from seeing it first hand that you can never fully clean up an oil spill like that. You simply contain the worst damage and give the appearance that it has been cleaned.'

'But surely that is an isolated case?' Camilla pulls her scarf tighter and shades herself from the wind.

'No way. There have been others that have not received as much media attention and some that have never been reported widely. But it's estimated there are several dozen spills a year world wide, and that adds up when you count the damage. Once you have seen it up close, you can never believe the PR spin again.' Sasha pulls her hood over her head.

'I reckon.' Cowrie focuses the binoculars as a cream and grey fulmar sweeps overhead and down near to the water, to glide back into a wind current and swoop up again. 'There's similar said about nuclear testing in the Pacific. That it's harmless, contained, can be cleaned up afterwards. The same sort of bullshit PR. But once you have visited Moruroa and seen it, you can never ever believe that crap again.'

'The worst thing,' suggests Monique, 'is that we may never know the full nature of the effects for a long time. How many oil spills have affected human and animal populations long term and what are their effects? The same with nuclear testing at Moruroa, throughout the Pacific and nuclear leaks all over Europe. The huge rise in cancer-related diseases is linked but this can seldom be conclusively proven, and where it is, the big boys' spin-doctors intervene.'

'I think you are all being too sensitive to the situation,' Camilla asserts. 'It is inevitable in a modern society that these accidents will happen, but we simply have to learn to live with them and do the best we can.'

Sasha intervenes. 'No, Camilla. We do not have to live with them. That is the party-line and what they want us to believe. But there are other ways of living and it's high time we matured enough to consider them instead of being threatened by them. My ancestors lived a sustainable existence without wiping out their or other species and there are plenty of models for doing this alongside modern technological developments. We simply need to think holistically to see the connections between the environment and how we live. It's not difficult. But it does require care and effort.'

Uretsete and DK emerge from below deck and point out the Island of Fara and the pier at Lyness, showing them the map, and explaining how they can get to see the Old Man of Hoy once they have landed. The huge Hoy Hills rise out of the sea and tower above, clouds moving fast across their belly, throwing shadows onto the island and dancing across the fields.

They hop back into the van to disembark and drive off the ferry, following the signposts to Rackwick, along a narrow road that is flanked by fields. Eventually they see an arrow pointing toward the Old Man of Hoy and park near the outdoor centre, walking the rest of the way. The path they take leads to a wee burn or stream, which ambles gently through a lush ravine where sweet smelling honeysuckle clings to wildflowers, bushes and ferns of fuschia, aspen, rowan, bracken, dog-rose and some varieties not mentioned in their guide book nor known to them yet.

After a while, they cross another stream and look further to see a waterfall with deliciously clear water. Sasha leads them upstream where they fill their bottles and taste the sweet waters of Hoy. 'To clean water and air and earth,' Sasha raises her bottle and they join her in a toast, except Camilla who prefers her thermos of Earl Grey. They return to the track and follow the signs to a small peaty path that slowly rises to the slopes of Moor Fea. DK insists they obey the signs literally at each of the kissing gates and kiss, while Camilla and Monique amuse themselves admiring the wildflowers, for which they both share a passion; Monique through the lens of her camera, and Camilla making brief sketches as they progress. They walk through heather and bracken as the path rounds until they see the ochre-red cliffs of Rora Head. They pause to watch the fulmars gliding on the wind and returning to their nests hidden in the crags of a vertical cliff.

Eventually, they make their way through abundant deer-grass along the narrow path until finally they are rewarded by their first glimpse of the huge rocky stack of stones that rises in a steep vertical cone 450 feet into the sky from a rugged shore, waves crashing around its base. The path lowers them down through alpine bearberry, cowberry and crowberry growing out of the rocky soils. They are flanked by the small Loch of Stourdale to their port and huge boulders to starboard and great skuas diving above, until the wild wind increases, warning them they are nearing the cliff edge, laced with marsh orchis and icelandic moss. Now, the vast cathedral spire of nature towers before them and the Old Man of Hoy glows in pink, red and ochre shades.

They are speechless, witnessing this magnificent sculpture created by the wind and sea working on the red sandstone of the cliffs of Hoy, reminding them of the twelfth century church of St Magnus they saw in Kirkwall shortly after arriving, with its pitted, sculpted, curving sandstone shapes. Both are living entities, full of spirit, one sculpted by sand and wind and sea and men, the other by nature alone.

They brace themselves against the wind as fulmars and skuas glide over their heads, in awe at the vast, towering skyscraper before them, little realising that a battle between life and death is now taking place in the humble seaside cottages they left earlier this morning.

That the links binding humans and nature are fast dissolving in the space between the place they lay their heads at night and the sea crashing into the Bay of Skaill below.

[21]

'Och, aye, he's as weighty as a sunken ship,' admits Squiddy, as he helps Morrigan haul the wounded seal off the back of the truck and into the old wheelbarrow. He looks up at them plaintively, moaning with pain as he is moved.

'Always was a bonnie wee lad,' Morrigan replies, as if he'd commented about a son rather than a seal.

Squiddy grins at her turn of phrase. He's always loved Morrigan like the son he didn't have, never mind her being a woman. She fished like a man, drank like a man, smoked like a man, and could haul up as many lobster creels as a man, so in Squiddy's eyes, that qualified her as a man. And she never indulged in that boring small talk of the women when they sat about drinking tea and eating oatcakes after the morning's housework. Squiddy hates gossip. It ruined his life and it nearly ruined Morrigan's and that would be enough to bind them had they not liked the same whisky and loved the same career as fishers to boot. He sighs, looking down into the bay and wishing he was out fishing today, despite the strong wind.

Morrigan holds the wheelbarrow carefully with the sick seal balanced inside and now propped up with blankets. Squiddy trots along beside her as she follows the rocky path from the cottages down to the far shed, once used for ploughs and tools when the land had been a working farmstead. Every now and again, Squiddy looks into the seal's eyes, wondering where he has seen that look before. He's spied many a seal, but none with eyes like this one, as green as the sea on a sunny day.

'Buggered if I know how yer gonna heal this seal, Morrigan.'

'It's useless letting those environmentalists look after it. They're as likely to treat him like a pet and he'll never be able to return to the sea,' replies Morrigan. 'No, far better he is in my care.'

'What'll yer do if he gives up the ghost, lassie?'

'I'll bury him here, Squiddy. Give him a decent send off where he can look out over the Bay of Skaill and hear his kin calling for him.'

'Have the others pulled through that you've tried to save?' asks Squiddy, who has helped Morrigan bring more than a few wounded seals back to the shed under the light of the moon or when nobody was about.

'Some've made it, a few've decided to lie at rest here in the bay,' replies Morrigan, looking out over the restless waves, hoping the seals will know he is safe with her.

Together, they carefully lift him from the barrow onto the sand which Morrigan always had piled up in the corner next to the door leading out to a farm pond, once used by cattle and sheep to drink from. 'He'll be as happy as a bull in a pile of hot shit here,' remarks Squiddy, rubbing his hands down his overalls and extracting some tobacco from his hip pocket to light up his pipe.

'Hope so.' Morrigan looks anxiously into the seal's eyes as she bends over him, stroking his head and neck. The seal looks up at Morrigan, begging her to continue. For a short moment in time, Squiddy wonders if there is some strange attraction between Morrigan and the seals — maybe she's into animals, y'know, in that weird kind of way? Some folks said so, coz she was always hanging about the seals, and she was different from the other girls. Never married, never had any boyfriend, except for

Kelpie. Then again, they said Kelpie was taken away by the seals, and his missus later on. You never could tell.

Squiddy puffs on his pipe, watching Morrigan tend to the seal more like it was her lover than a fish-stealing mammal. Takes all types, I s'pose, he reckons, and buggered if I care what anybody does in their own time, so long as they act friendly in the pub, fish fair and get along with their mates. Morrigan's a good sort, for sure. He dismisses the errant thoughts, as if they have never crossed his mind, and peers out the empty stone window frame, across the barley hills and down into the Bay of Skaill.

[22]

A dark cloud obscures their vision for a few moments, until the sun breaks through and penetrates the upper levels of the water, revealing the squid propelling themselves forward by their small, powered jet-packs. Sandy skims up and catches one in his mouth, only to get a face full of ink spat out at him as the squid's protection. Fiona laughs, pulling some succulent seafood from under the toothed wrack kelp, their shells breaking easily between her teeth. Emerging from a cloud of ink, Sandy still holds the struggling squid between his teeth and looks triumphant as he wolfs down the wriggling fish head first so its tentacles cannot propel it forward again.

After he has finished eating the squid, Sandy dives down to greet Fiona amid the saw wrack and dabber-locks swinging gently in the current. 'Yee turning vege-tarian again, Fe? Yee'll never survive the winter just nibbling seaweed. Yee need some good fleshy halibut and sea salmon to sustain the next season.'

'Yee eat too much of that Sandy. Yee could do with some nutritious kelp. There's nothing more luscious than a taste of crinkled, frilly sugar kelp on a warm sunny day, or a bite of that delicate, olivy, ferny leaf of dabberlocks. I remember seeing it near the low water line in my Nofin days and now I regret never having the courage to taste it then. Yee need more greens.' Fiona tugs at another frond of the toothed wrack, keen to savour the spiral seashells that cling to its underbelly, floating the first leaf over to Sandy and taking the second for herself.

'Do yee know who it was caught in the fisherman's

net last week, Fe?' asks Sandy, watching as the kelp floats slowly past his nose.

Fiona glances up from her intense concentration on finding the small spiral seasnails, 'I have no idea, Sandy, but I'm sure we would've heard if it had been any of our clan, now, would we not?'

'Sure enough, Fe. Then again, not all the deaths have been noticed of late. So many from floating plastic and nets and did I tell yee about that time when some school-boys battered one of our young 'uns to death? They'd heard their fisherfolk complaining about us seals eating all their fish and the father had mentioned it was a pity the days of clubbing were over. The young lads got it into their heads it'd be fun to club the poor creature to death and they battered her with stones found at the beach until they were all covered in blood. Some grey seals watched it from their wee skerry off the coast and they were horrified. They never let any of their clan near that beach again, remaining on the skerry or out at sea.'

'How did yee know about their motives, Sandy?'

'A week later, some grey seals pulled the father of one of the boys into the sea and he admitted what he had said. They asked him if he would like to be a seal for two years without any possibility of returning. They would not grant him selkie status until he had earned it. He refused, so they let him float to the bottom of the sea. It's said he tasted like a fish, he'd eaten so many of our relatives, like a big, rotting jellyfish covered in beer batter. He liked his ale, did Jimmy McDonald.' He laughs.

Fiona wrinkles up her sealy nose. 'You can talk, Sandy. I bet yee'd taste the same right now. Like a slithery squid, with squiddy ink flowing through your selkie skin.' She flicks her tale flukes near his belly to emphasise her point.

'Not as nasty as slithery seaweed, rotting in your gut, all curling around inside you like a mad seasnake in the stomach of a vegetarian selkie.' Sandy wrinkles up his whiskers, enjoying teasing her.

Fiona drops the kelp she is nibbling and it floats gently to the sea floor. She fixes her eyes onto Sandy. 'Yee just wait. I'll make sure yee regret that.' She swoops up and knocks him sideways, then dives into the kelp bed which she knows so well now. He flicks his tail and dives after her, but it takes him some time to catch up. Fiona weaves her way skilfully through the thick tangle and edges under a ledge she figures he will not know about. Sandy glides past gleefully, thinking he is hot on her trail and will catch her the next corner he rounds. She chuckles to herself. Then she notices the shape circling above and sending dark shadows onto the seafloor below. It is a great white shark and it is moving in the direction Sandy has swum. Sandy has rounded the rock ledge and she cannot see him. The shark swims steadily forward, edging its way slowly as it contemplates the easy prey ahead.

[23]

'Set into the floor, near the hearth, are stone boxes, the joints of which are luted, or cemented with clay, to make them watertight. It is likely they were used to soak limpets so they are soft enough to be used for fish bait.' DK eyes the cute young woman who guides them through the ancient seaside village, wondering if she is a dyke. She has a labrys earring made from silver and wears a waist coat over a silk shirt. Her hair is cut short and spiky.

'Calling DK. Back to earth, DK,' Uretsete breathes into her ear. 'Check out these limpet boxes. They must have used them in rotation since they have several smaller ones rather than one large box. Maybe we could try the same and see what we can catch from the rocks off Skara Brae?' DK is too busy checking out whether the boots are Doc Martens or some local variety to reply.

'Note the central hearth in each house. This was essential for warmth and fuel was probably a mixture of dung, heather, bracken, marine mammal bone which is rich in oil, and dried seaweed.' The guide points towards the hearth, adding that what wood may have been available was too precious to burn and was most likely kept for tool making.

Cowrie is busy looking closely at the carvings on the walls of the houses and passages linking them. The guide notes that the designs are abstract and have no meaning known to archeologists but did for the artists at the time. Cowrie peers at the two stones nearest her. They both have etchings similar to those on the ki'i pohaku or rock drawings found on cave walls in Hawai'i and Aotearoa.

There the drawings depict animals and birdpeople and more recognisable figures, but here the lines are like the journeys described by scratches on the pahoehoe or lava rock with diagonals and crosses marking sites of interest. Aboriginals in Australia marked such sites with spiral and circular designs painted onto bark or etched in the sand or rock. A pity so many archeologists work only from their monocultural knowledge, thinks Cowrie, taking out a sketch pad to jot down the neolithic designs etched into the walls of the Skara Brae houses.

'How come the village was preserved so well, and how did knowledge of it become known?' asks a tartan-clad Scotsman, peering over his half-spectacles, his rich red eyebrows raised in expectation.

'It was the winter of 1850,' explains the guide. 'A wild storm stripped the grass from the top of the dunes revealing an immense midden or refuse heap and the first glimpses of these ancient dwellings.'

'How old are they?' his wife asks, leaning on his shoulder.

'Skara Brae was inhabited before the Egyptian pyramids were built and the community here flourished many centuries before work began on constructing Stonehenge. The original village, on which this now stands, was built about 5000 BCE and this one was inhabited about 3100 BCE to 2500 BCE.'

'Awesome,' says DK, referring to the embossed silver bangle the guide wears, where two seahorses erupt from two globes under which lie two celtic crosses. The crowd murmurs in assent, thinking she is admiring the houses, not discovering a partially closet Orcadian mermaid.

'But how did they begin? I mean the houses are so strongly structured and have lasted 5000 years.'

'They are built on refuse essentially,' explains the

guide, moving her hand out of DK's vision. The people living in the earlier village under Skara Brae collected their refuse in a midden made from shells, broken bones, ash, stone and organic material. Together, it makes for strong building material. When enough of it is gathered, then they dug mounds in it and built stone linings inside the mounds for walls. The subterranean design kept away the strong Orcadian winds and sea salt and they built huge roof structures overtop from whalebone gathered from the beaches and covered with skins and natural fibres.'

'Ingenious. Bloody ingenious,' mutters the clan-man puffing on his pipe.

Cowrie is by now examining the tools used by the villagers and found during the excavations. There are several bone points, from stranded whales, some with holes in the top, probably used for stitching skins. They'd also be excellent for drawing out lobster and crabmeat, thinks Cowrie, the juices in her mouth gathering at the thought. This was clearly a part of their diet from the archeological digs and midden remains. An impressive bone awl made from the leg-bone of a gannet is carved to a perfect point. Pots made of stone, bone and oyster shells and containing dried ochre may have been for skin painting or for decorating carvings.

She moves to examine the jewellery, mostly marine-mammal bone pendants, in the shape of shark's teeth and a huge number of beads and bone pins. She nudges Uretsete. 'Hey, check these out, sister. Looks like some of your cuzzie-bros came this way too.' She points to the jewellery which could have come from a coastal Chumash or Miwok village. Some of the pins are from walrus tusks, common in Orkney at the time. One of the pins has a dark, burnt texture, from heating the bone carefully, its effect similar to pit-fired pottery. The hand carving is beautiful, though none of it as complex or intricate as Maori bone carvings nor Celtic work. Nevertheless, impressive, as Uretsete agrees.

'We can deduce from the archeological evidence,' continues the guide, 'that the Skara Brae village was egalitarian. The houses are similar in size and structure and thus no chiefs requiring larger premises were here. The house structures show a community bound by strong beliefs and able to live communally. There are no defensive structures and among all the tools and objects found in middens, there were absolutely no weapons whatsoever at Skara Brae, leading us to conclude that these were not warring people.'

'Amazing. I like it,' murmurs Uretsete and several agree with her.

'Nowhere else in Europe can we see such rich evidence of how our ancestors truly lived. I hope you have found this tour of Skara Brae inspiring and I will be here to answer any further questions.' The guide ends her spiel and is surrounded by eager questioners.

Uretsete examines the artist's drawings of the roofs of the houses, from the evidence gathered, and is amazed to see that there is little or no ventilation provided and that the archeologists assumed that the houses were very smoky. She reads the inscription: 'There would have been little ventilation. The air inside the houses would have been very smoky.' She points this out to Cowrie, asking her to recall the Miwok village she visited near Tomales Bay in California when they first met. 'Didn't Peta take you to the old village,' she asks, 'and you would have seen the deer-skin flap over the teepee roof to let out air when there was a fire. It is likely it was very similar here. They could never survive in smoke-filled underground rooms all winter. Some of these archies really take the cake!'

Cowrie laughs. 'Yep, you'd think they could piece that together.'

Meantime, DK has been working her charms on the delightful guide and after the visitors have left to return to their coach, she asks if it would be all right to wander about some more. Kerry, as she is called, says it is fine and, if they have any further questions to ask her, she will be in the cafe. They explore the village again, delighting in imagining the community which must have lived here, then join Kerry in the Skara Brae restaurant. DK buys her a second baked tattie filled with delicious tomatoes and local Swanney cheese melted on the top, and they ask her whether it is likely a group of women ever lived here alone.

'Officially, no. It appears that there was a family settlement here. But the lack of weapons and hierarchy certainly makes me wonder, unless they lived a more matriarchal lifestyle,' she offers, looking around to make sure none of the staff have heard her. 'There are many local tales about the mythical women of Skara Brae, but they can never be proved nor disproved. One thing is for sure, they lived a peaceful existence and one based around ritual and ceremonies held at the Ring of Brodgar and Stenness. They killed only enough seafood or animals to survive and it's likely they collected herbs, wild plants, fruits and nuts for eating, and maybe baked their own bread since they grew wheat and barley. The temperatures were warmer than today, lucky devils,' she adds, with a grin.

'Is it true that two elderly women were found buried in the walls of one of the houses? If so, why?' asks Cowrie.

Kerry rests her fork on her plate a moment, looks into

the far distance, and sighs. 'I never know how to answer this,' she admits, 'but it's true. It is clear that this was an intentional burial, and we know that many ceremonial burials took place, mainly for important chiefs and the like at Maes Howe and throughout Britain. But why these women were interred in the walls of a humble community house is another question.'

'Maybe it was like that foundation ritual where Saint Columba buried one of his monks to found the church on Iona?' suggests DK, recalling their recent visit to the sacred island.

'It's highly possible', replies Kerry, 'especially since similar practices lasted in the UK into the seventh century, long after Skara Brae was built.'

'Maybe they were ancestors and were blessed by the tribe for some reason. Perhaps they saved the community from some disaster and became ancestral spirits or guardians who were consulted for spiritual matters and guidance. That's common in my tribe also and not beyond belief here.'

'That is very possible,' answers Kerry. 'I even heard one of the archeologists suggest this, but she later added that she could never write it up in her reports because she would be accused of speculating rather than sticking to facts alone.'

'Typical. A bit more imagination and some cross-cultural work could elucidate some of the inscriptions here now,' Uretsete suggests.

'Were there any male burials found?' asks DK.

'No, come to think of it, none at all. That's what has fuelled speculation it was an entirely peaceful and close-knit female community.' Kerry resumes work on her baked tattie.

Another hour is spent eagerly imagining what life may

have been like at Skara Brae over a selection of seafood and baked tatties, then they depart for home. DK thanks Kerry for giving so much beyond her duty and she replies, 'It's a pleasure to find people so genuinely interested. Most of the tourists simply come, take a few pictures and depart, and you know their main experience of Orkney will be buying mugs inscribed with Orkney names or plastic puffins.' They laugh, knowing what she means, but assuring her that many of the people will think about this experience again one day over a cuppa back in Dundee or Yorkshire, Montreal or Melbourne. A van, similar to Morrigan's, draws up and whisks her away before DK can deduce whether it is driven by a man or a woman.

'Damn! I'll have to come back again,' mumbles DK.

'And so will I,' adds Uretsete, nudging her affectionately.

DK grins, knowing she is lucky to be with Uretsete and glad that her former lover Ruth went off to live on a kibbutz in Israel about the time DK's lover, Suzanne, was called back south to look after her ailing parents. At first, they'd cried on each other's shoulders, missing their loved ones intensely. Then gradually they cuddled up for the night and eventually became lovers after the Miwok village summer solstice, when they went to celebrate the expansion of the Tomales Bay oyster farms run by Uretsete's relatives.

DK looks out over the Bay of Skaill, uncharacteristically calm today, remembering that wonderful night when the moon shone over Tomales Bay and lit up their faces as they kissed by the shoreline. A seal swam by and issued a throaty cry, as if announcing their love. She scans the horizon. Not a seal in sight. They must be munching on kelp below, she thinks, as they put on their packs to climb the hill up to the cottages.

Above them, smoke issues from the shed at the far end of Morrigan's farm. Cowrie notices it, and is surprised. She had thought it was a disused shed. She must ask Morrigan who lives there.

[24]

Wind and rain pound against the roof and they have to batten it down with large stones at the side.

The fire keeps them warm and the women gather around the hearth. Their faces are painted with ochre and strings of beads decorated with limpet shells hang around their necks. One necklace has a black mussel shell in the middle, another a carved deer-bone. Some of the women are painting shells and others are painting bodies with crosses and spirals. Still more work at carving grooves into pots they are preparing to fire in the central hearth. In a corner, one woman turns the limpets in their watery graves.

Gradually, a slow chant begins from the left and moves around the circle to the right.

A woman holds up some dried herbs bound together with heather twine and dips it into the limpet water to slow the burning and make it smoke more, then lights it from the roaring fire. The smoke rises to the roof where an opening on an angle to prevent rain from coming through allows it to disappear into the moist night air.

The chanting of the women rises in pitch and they stand around the circle, eyes closed, deep in concentration. Then they turn, as if one, and face the wall. The voices rise higher in pitch until they are soaring above the room and out into the bay. They never once take their concentration from the wall. Finally, one of the women steps forward and asks a question. After a while, a voice replies, from within the wall. The chanting continues, quietly, and the questions go on for some time. Another voice answers.

110

Eventually, the painted woman steps back into the circle. There is a hushed silence as she communicates the message. A great sand storm is to come within the next few seasons, and before the summer. They have been warned to move out from the village. They will assume a new lifestyle, returning to the old mode of living in individual homes. They will be isolated again, for a period. But they will find each other and live communally again if they want to. It is up to them. Other women will come and live in the Bay in years to come. They will also feel the energy of the work that has taken place here. They will tune into it and tell the true stories of a matriarchal existence that once happened here. They will tell about the secrets of the seals, the oneness of human and animals, that to kill another is to kill oneself. The women of Skara Brae will always return in different shapes and forms until the world is healed again and peace is restored.

After she has communicated the words from the women elders, the women turn to the wall and thank them for their wisdom. Some are crying. They do not want to be parted and nor do they want to leave Skara Brae and join the mens' community over the loch. Maybe others will build on top of their homes as they did on their ancestors' homes? Anything is possible.

A screeching from outside as an oystercatcher is blown into their roof. Cowrie wakes with a start to find that Sasha is fast asleep beside her and it is still light outside. She carefully slides out of bed and walks quietly to the window facing the bay. From the shed at the end of the farm, smoke rises. Far beyond, waves lap against the wall below the buried village of Skara Brae. She stays a while at the window, watching as the early morning mists gather around the bay and move up the hillside, then she puts on her clothes. It is unlikely she will get back to sleep now and she wants to find out who lives in the shed at the end of the farm where the smoke swirls from the old chimney day and night.

Cowrie steals out into the cold morning air. It is freezing. She shudders, pulling her oilskin tighter and wrapping her scarf twice around her neck. The ground is wet and the heather crunches beneath her feet. She moves to the narrow dirt path once made by cattle and continues down the track. She stops before the shed and listens to assess if people are about. All she can hear is the steady roll of the surf crashing onto the rocks in the bay below and a slow moaning, like an animal in pain. She creeps slowly towards the window and stands on a rock to peer inside. At first all she can see is hay and she smells a foul odour of oil. Then she makes out a creature moaning in the distance. She peers closer, dislodging a stone from the mound she is standing on. The creature looks up at her with plaintive eyes. Maybe it is a dying cow. It is too dark to see inside distinctly.

A shuffling outside and someone walks in from the far wall carrying what appears to be a bucket. He tips water all over the animal and then leaves to fetch another. This goes on several times until he bends down in exhaustion over the animal, murmuring. Cowrie stretches up to see better, dislodging another stone which tumbles down the pile and rolls over, kicking the wall. The figure scrambles up and goes toward the door. Cowrie lies flat against the wall, hoping he will not see her. He mumbles something indistinct and then shuts the door, pulling down the latch to secure it. He then returns to the moaning creature and bends over it as before. It's then that she hears the words. 'My darling, sweet darling, do not give up on me now. I have waited so long for you to return and you cannot die now. Just let me stay with you and you can return and be with me forever.' The voice is that of Morrigan. She must have really lost it, poor thing. At that moment, the creature moans again, as if trying to answer her and flicks its tail up in the air. It is no cow's tail, nor that of a sheep. It is the tail of a seal, and Morrigan is now crooning into its ear as if the seal is her lover. She gently strokes the seal, touching her with such grace and affection that Cowrie wonders if she is still inside her Skara Brae dream.

She has had little sleep tonight and maybe she is hallucinating. She clambers down from the rock ledge and walks briskly back to the cottage, flinging off her clothes and climbing back into bed beside Sasha, cuddling up to her. Sasha moans briefly, then falls back into sleep. Within minutes, Cowrie follows her into dreamland, and is snoring happily several hours later when Sasha rises.

'C'mon Cowrie. It's nearly ten. We're off to the Broch of Gurness, remember? The others will be waiting for us.'

Cowrie raises herself up on one arm, rubbing her eyes. 'What? When? My head feels like lead.'

'That's because you slept too late, Turtle. Besides, you talked some weird nonsense in your sleep and I simply rolled you over and went back to sleep myself.'

'What did I say?' asks Cowrie, recalling her dreams about the women of Skara Brae, then of visiting the hut.

'Something about wounded seals and women chanting. I could not make it out so I dozed off.'

'I had some awesome dreams.'

'Tell me later, Turtle. Just fling on some clothes and follow me out.' Sasha throws her the jacket and trousers at the bottom of the bed, noticing they are covered in

113

mud, yet they were freshly washed the day before. Maybe Cowrie has been on some night jaunts? She chuckles at the thought of her going anywhere in the state she was in last night and exits out the door to join the others. Cowrie stares at the clothes, realising that she did indeed venture out and that maybe what she saw really did happen? Maybe Morrigan has some weird thing with seals after all? She dismisses the thought from her head and finds clean clothes to wear. As she shuts the door, she cannot resist a glance down to the shed. Sure enough, smoke still smoulders from the chimney and she will not be surprised to hear from Camilla that Morrigan has not yet come home.

Sasha leads the singing as they drive towards the Broch of Gurness, happy to have the use of Morrigan's van all this time. She left a note for Camilla telling them to use it as she'd be away for at least a week with some Finstown fishers, keen to see what catches lay further afield. Squiddy would collect her in his truck. Camilla was not pleased but took it as a good chance to get some thorough cleaning and polishing done while Morrigan was well out of the way, little realising she was holed up with supplies and a sick seal in the shed further down the farm.

'How did that Maori song you taught us in California go?' asks Uretsete. 'You know, the one where the strong women gather round and encourage each other to stay strong.'

'Wahine ma, wahine ma, maranga mai, maranga mai, kia kaha!' Cowrie's spirit rises as she bursts into the waiata at the top of her voice and repeats the round so the others can learn it. Gather round women, join together, stay strong.' Soon the van is resounding with songs from their own repertoires and Cowrie even joins Camilla for rousing renditions of Land of Hope and Glory and Jerusalem, though she recalls having refused to sing such patriotic colonial songs at school. Sasha teaches them an Inuit chant which is captivating but uses a different tonal range which they have to learn carefully from her. Soon they have figured it out and Uretsete is amazed at the similarities to some of her own Chumash and Miwok songs in melody, tone and pace. They compare notes while the others sing heartily, pleased to be off on another exploration of these extraordinary islands which hold so many secrets to our shared past lives.

They drive through Dounby then pass by the Click Mill and the delightful town of Evie, where campers from the local campsite are stocking up on supplies, then turn left on the narrow road leading down to the sea and to the Broch of Gurness. DK reads to them from the guidebook about the history of the brochs in Orkney. The Orcadians were building strong circular dry-stone houses on their farms by 500 BCE during the Iron Age and gradually they became more sophisticated with villages sprouting around them. Some were as tall as thirteen metres high with chambers around the edges and a stone staircase leading up to a higher level, and were used as central gathering places for the communities as well as a kind of castle where they could keep an eye on the surrounding countryside and the possibility of invaders approaching. By 100 BCE there were at least one hundred and twenty brochs in Orkney and about five hundred over Scotland, but none were found demolished by violent destruction rather than wear and tear, leading to the conclusion that the Orcadians lived a fairly peaceful existence even by the Iron Age.

'I find it inspiring that wherever we go, it seems that history shows us the natural inhabitants lived peacefully here, even though they were constantly invaded by outsiders like the Vikings later on,' comments Monique, eager to understand how the people lived from the archeological evidence.

Camilla reinforces her impressions, telling them that it is clear from her reading of the Orkneyinga Saga, written in 1200, that the brochs were used as a mutual deterrent since any attack on them would lead to many deaths which the working population on these islands could not afford. Also the archeological evidence shows that the outer ditches and walls designed for defence were built over, indicating there was little need for them.

They park and walk to the Broch of Gurness and are inspired by its location beside the sea with the waves crashing in at their feet. The broch still stands as an impressive rounded structure of stone, with walls crumbled part the way up and hearths, beds and living evidence of the inhabitants still intact, though not as much as at Skara Brae. The broch and surrounding village structures grow out of the stark green grass, as if an organic part of nature.

'Who took over after the Iron Age inhabitants?,' asks Uretsete and DK scans her book.

'The Picts, from all accounts. Carved stones and Pictish writings called ogham show there was a thriving Pictish settlement here and in other parts of Orkney.'

They explore the impressive ruins in their picturesque setting beside the sea, as the sun works hard to break through the clouds. It is a misty morning and the sea is uncharacteristically calm, giving a haunting feeling to the ruins as they keep watch over the Holy Island of Eynhallow and the seaside Broch of Midhowe on the nearby island of Rousay. It is possible to imagine life here in the Iron Age and people bustling about the broch. Like Skara Brae, the stone structures had timber and whalebone roofs covered with skins, hearths, storage pits and wall cupboards in the stone, but here there is also a water well.

Pit-fired pottery, bone weaving combs, a Pictish knife with a bone handle carved with ogham script, and hand-made bronze pins all tell of a community rich with skills and from remains it seems the gathering of seaweed, shellfish and wild plants complemented the early farming of cattle on the island and the weaving of clothes from sheep and goat's wool. Cowrie examines the Pictish script and drawings closely. Again, the archeological experts are stumped on their meaning, but like the ki'i pohaku or inscriptions in lava rock and on cave walls in Hawai'i and Aotearoa, they depict ordinary aspects of Pictish life rather than the expectation of modern art that it is separate from and better than common existence.

One stone shows a woman with a halo around her head, typical of the early Hawai'ian drawings, a V marking her chest, standing opposite a man. Next to her, by its size, lies the grave of a child. Perhaps they are mourning the death of their child. Maybe the woman's spirit, marked by the halo, will guide that of her child as it makes the journey of transition, just as the spirit guides live inside the pohutukawa tree at the tip of Cape Reinga in her homeland, waiting to guide dead spirits back over the seas to their ancestral homeland in Hawai'iki. People usually comment in script, talkstory or drawing when something touches their lives, and it is from this heart place that the archeologists need to look as well as from their reasoning head place.

Cowrie allows herself to imagine what was going through that woman's head at the time, wondering if the women elders interred in the walls of Skara Brae spoke to these Iron-age women and the later Viking women in their dreams as well. The sea laps at the edges of the stony beach and Sasha lays a hand on her shoulder. 'Back to earth yet, Turtle?' Cowrie looks up to notice she is as far away in thought over the sea as Cowrie was in dreamspace. 'A pity Morrigan is not here as she might be able to tell us more about the Broch of Midhowe on Rousay.' Sasha looks longingly at the broch on the island opposite them.

'Bet you wish you had your kayak here now, eh, Sasha?' Cowrie asks. Sasha grins. 'But talking of Morrigan, I had an amazing dream about the women of Skara Brae last night and also about Morrigan. Only I got up and checked the shed and you will not believe what I saw.'

Sasha looks into her dark brown eyes affectionately. 'Tell me, Turtle. I know you went out adventuring last night and now I want to hear all about it.' Cowrie is relieved to be able to share her doubts about Morrigan and have Sasha reassure her all is well. After she has finished telling her about the dream and the night visit, Sasha sighs. 'I think it all has a perfectly clear explanation. Morrigan already rescued a sick seal, the one you told me you saw at Stromness through the binoculars that day. She's a very private person and especially when it comes to anything sentimental or which will show her as the caring woman that she really is underneath that butch exterior. It makes sense to me that she would not tell us that she is going to give up her fishing livelihood and her independence for a week to nurse a sick seal back to health. She probably feels guilt if it got caught in her net, and unlike the other fishers, she does not see the seals as competitors for her catch.'

'She uses lobster creels, not nets. And besides, that does not explain the intimate words she whispered to the seal. I found that strange and weird.'

'Maybe she knew the seal in its human form?'

'What do you mean by that?'

'Just what I said, Turtle.'

'So that might explain why she is being so secretive about it?'

'Maybe, or simply that she does things her way. That would be typical of Morrigan too. Now let's leave her to her work, unless she asks for our help, and let her be. I think our energies will be better spent exploring this fascinating land and working towards the storytelling festival.'

'Too true.' Cowrie cuddles into Sasha and they perch on the edge of a stone seat, looking out over the awesome remains of the broch and into the wild currents swirling about in the Eynhallow channel and sweeping by Rousay. 'I wouldn't like to be caught in a kayak in that whirlpool of currents,' admits Cowrie.

'Me neither,' replies Sasha, folding her arm around Cowrie's shoulder and warming her against the cold wind blowing in from the sea and ruffling the once calm waters off Gurness.

After the others have explored Gurness to their heart's content, they walk around the rocks to the sands of Evie. Here, a sandy beach stretches out as far as the eye can see. Sasha presses her fingers tight around Cowrie's hand. 'Just like Aotearoa, eh Turtle?'

'Except for the weather,' jokes Cowrie and they slowly start gathering empty spoot shells lying in abundance amidst the seaweed and driftwood piled up on the sand. Soon all are finding new shells to absorb them and there is a surprising abundance of brightly coloured shells in amongst the ever present large limpets. Orange and yellow and brown spiral shells, purple sea eggs worn down by the waves so that their once spiky outsides are just round ridges, tiny black and purple mussel shells, smaller than they have ever seen, a conical shell with brown swirls around the sides leading up to a perfect tip.

'Turtle, come here. You won't believe what I have just found.' Sasha holds up an elongated shell as tiny as a fingernail, creamy white with grooved ridges around. She turns it over to reveal a line of teeth leading into a mysterious interior, hidden from the naked eye. It is a minute cowrie shell, smaller than she has ever seen and totally different from the rich brown turtle-shell markings of the Pacific cowries, covering over a bright purple interior shell. Cowrie turns it over in her hand marvelling at the beauty of this small and distant cousin to her own shells, too tiny to put up to your ear and hear the murmurings of the sea. Sasha had found it under a pile of tangle, so they search under more seaweed and find a total of nine cowries, all of them as minute. The others gather round and Cowrie hands the shells out to them.

'What'll you do with the others, Turtle?' asks Sasha.

'One each goes back home for Mere, Kuini and Maata. The last one is for Morrigan. When she returns from fishing,' she adds, looking over to Camilla, and thinking that Morrigan might need all the protection afforded traditionally by the cowrie shell. She hopes she'll be able to sing her waiata through this cowrie, bring the Orcadian woman back into her true self and love, whatever that is, as she did with young Sahara.

Infused with a new challenge, and inspired by the final breaking through of the sun, Cowrie flings off her layers of clothes with ostentatious pleasure, much to the shock of a few English birdwatchers, replete with binoculars and very heavily clad in winter woollies themselves, and runs into the waves. She dives and takes in a gulp of seawater, her body shocked at the icy cold. Camilla averts her eyes and Monique watches in awe, but Sasha, DK and Uretsete, taking this as a challenge, throw off layer after layer of clothing and rush to be next into the ocean, screaming with glee as they hit the freezing waters.

The English couple try to ignore them, focusing on the oystercatchers trying to dig for spoots, but they cannot pretend it is not happening once three more bodies dive naked into the sea. The woman leans over to her husband, whose binoculars are now pinned on the large, luscious naked bodies, his eyes bulging in secret behind his glasses. 'Really, Reginald, I have no idea why these young women have to flaunt themselves so eagerly. It's disgusting. It's time we moved on.' She gathers her thermos, scarf, binoculars and camera and heads for the Volvo parked by the road.

Reginald, far from wanting to move, murmurs 'yes, dear' and focuses his binoculars more clearly so he can see the bulging breasts of these brown and cream Botticelli bodies playing in the surf like mermaids. 'Go for it. Enjoy your youth while you have it,' he mumbles to himself. 'Reginald, come immediately,' yells out Mrs Reginald from the car park. 'You have the keys and I cannot get in.' Reginald sighs, rubs his penis unobtrusively, as if it were once a living organism, and obediently returns to the car.

Oblivious to this pantomime, acted out all over the once powerful Empire on various stages and in various guises, the mermaids frolic and play, diving and leaping around in the water, none wanting to be the first to scramble up the beach for the protection of warm clothes again. Cowrie is the first in and the first out. She rushes across the sand and in the distance, notices a silver Volvo taking off from the carpark with rapid motion. 'Great,' she yells, 'we have the beach to ourselves and the sea creatures.' She turns around to wave to the others and notices a lone seal out on the horizon, hovering in the waters, its head looking inland as if searching for someone.

[26]

Fiona waits tensely flicking her tail back and forward in the shadow of the rocky ledge as the great white shark skims past her in pursuit of Sandy, who has disappeared around the edge of the rocky outcrop. She dare not move for fear of being seen by the shark, yet she wants to distract his attention from Sandy. She notices a few squid in the upper waters and wonders if she can reach them in time. When the shark circles around, moving with his back toward her, she darts out and up, grabbing a squid in her mouth. Immediately it squirts a jet of blacky blue ink at her and she dives toward the shark directly. Just as the squid prepares to squirt her again, she thrusts it in front of the shark, clouding his vision for a moment. She darts down toward Sandy, but he has already gone.

The shark emerges from the mist and turns toward her, slashing his tail maliciously. She swiftly swims back toward the ledge. He pursues her with all the force of his large and strong body, more than three lengths her size. He opens his huge jaws ready for the crunch. Terrified, she slips in under the ledge just in time and he wraps his jaws around a jagged rock covered in oysters which rip the sides of his mouth. He turns away, flicking his tail angrily and sending a school of mackerel darting for a quick escape in all directions. His mouth is bleeding and his body is rigid with anger. Oyster scratches are the most painful shellfish cuts of all, especially about the mouth area. He surges back in the direction he was pursuing Sandy, going three times the speed the fittest seal could manage. Fiona's heart pounds in her stomach, sending shivers out to the very tips of her fins. She has done all she can to divert the great white. It is up to fate from now on. All she can do is send vibrations through the water to warn Sandy.

[27]

The purplish-black mussels sizzle on the peat fire, opening in the heat and drizzling their juices down onto the cockles cooking below. Eager mouths wait as Cowrie cooks the last batch of seafood on the flames and hands it round in clay bowls for all to sample. Camilla has made a delicious mustard and cress salad with sliced cucumber and Monique added a blue cheese sauce dripping lusciously over mushrooms at the top, spiced up by a few purple wildflowers she's found in the field on Morrigan's land. They feel magnificent after a day out in the fresh air and a shockingly cold but refreshing swim off the sands of Evie.

Later in the afternoon, they'd collected mussels from the rocks on the way home and dug for cockles and for razors. The spoots had mostly eluded them, only a few falling victim to their backward steps over the flats, and they'd felt it worthy of a feast in honour of the citizens of the Broch of Gurness, who'd revealed treasures from their lives by leaving behind monuments that would stand the test of time for future generations to see. Monique begins a game of suggesting what, from their own disposable culture, would be around 5000 years later, like Skara Brae, and in the span between the Iron Age and now.

'A midden of smashed computers,' suggests DK. 'And I doubt if Bill Gates'd be the first to dig holes in 'em to hollow out a space for his new stone house.' They laugh, visualising the Skara Brae building methods used with modern rubbish heaps.

'A thousand inflated condoms tied together would

make an excellent roof,' suggests Camilla, delighted to be relaxed enough to offer a joke rather than shunning theirs. They grimace at the thought but enjoy the madness of it too.

'I'd go for the traditional shellfish middens, myself,' offers Cowrie, tucking into a second helping of sweet fresh cockles tasting of peat smoke and sea salt. 'I could live inside that midden and simply use the old shells to build the next house on top, like the women of Skara Brae.'

'Reckon I'd come and join you.' Monique has never been into shellfish much in Frankfurt and has discovered she loves it fresh from the sea, and that her West Indian ancestors probably feasted on it in Trinidad too. Her grandfather had come to Germany in the First World War and stayed to marry a Frankfurt woman. Their relationship had broken many taboos at the time and she recalls her grandmother telling of how she wheeled Monique's mother in a pram as a baby and was spat on in the street.

She'd grown up with West-Indian/German parents who tried to assimilate as much as possible after the Nazi regime and who talked seldom about their relatives back home in the West Indies. She'd had to press them for information and longed to visit her cousins one day to see for herself the heritage and country she came from. She grew up as a black German, a breed apart, with no status, rights nor respect, unlike the American Blacks who'd fought for their freedom and at least won some token respect.

One night she'd shared this with the group and it had been the first time she had ever voiced her desire to return to Trinidad. She'd never liked Germany but knew no other place she could call home. Now her English is good enough, she will make the trip for sure. Just tasting the shellfish reminds her of smells and sounds and tastes she's had in her mouth since she was born and could never explain since she had never actually tasted the shellfish nor breadfruit nor watermelon before. Now she knows it is a memory ingrained in her, an inherited tradition she is being called to explore.

'Monique, hand over the mussels, girl. That's the third time I've asked.' Sasha nudges her as she passes the shellfish, still inside her dreamspace. 'I'd go for a broch made of pure, clean ice right now,' continues Sasha, 'and to the right of the hearth in the middle, I'd carve a hole in the ice to fish through. I'd haul up the fish and land them straight onto the fire. Now you couldn't get fresher than that.' She grins, enjoying playing on the stereotypically eskimo imagery that most people imagine when they first meet an Inuit person, even though she has grown up in huts rather than igloos and with fish from the local store rather than the sea, until her father taught her the ancient skills of kayak fishing.

Camilla grimaces. 'Well, it all sounds fine for you but horrible for the fish. I'd rather stay with my sprouts and beans.'

'Howd'yer know they don't hurt when you pull them out,' ventures DK, playing devil's advocate. 'I recall reading about Mandrake Roots in early English poetry and how they screamed and shrieked when you dragged them out of the ground. Maybe sprouts have hearts too. Maybe they hurt when you force feed them all that water then munch them alive.'

Camilla puts her hands over her ears. DK grins and says she is only teasing but Camilla can no longer hear her.

'Okay, you two, give it up.' Uretsete suggests instead

that they settle into an evening of storytelling and starts off by telling them about how Hutash created the Rainbow Bridge so that the people on the Island of Carpinteria could walk across to the mainland of Great Turtle Island, once the population boomed, and how some looked down and fell into the waters below, turning into dolphins. Now everyone respects and loves dolphins, knowing that some of their relatives may be those swimming past today.

Cowrie recalls her lover Peta telling her this story and how deeply affected she was by it, and remembers the dream where Peta fell into the water and became a dolphin, swimming off with another dolphin, and how it predicted Peta's relationship with Nanduye. Now Sasha is descended from the dolphins too. Maybe there is something to this? Maybe it's not so strange to think of Morrigan's closeness to the seals. After all, it is Laukiamanuikahiki, Turtle Woman, who has offered Cowrie protection all these years, brought her back to Hawai'i in search of her lost roots and sent her out into the wild oceans to rediscover her own true wave-length.

Camilla tells an enchanting tale about MacCodrum of the Seals which her Scottish grandmother told her, and for the first time they realise she has Scottish as well as English roots.

It is a long story beginning with the King and Queen of the sea dwelling below the waves in happiness with their lovely sea-children, who had seaweed hair and played with the seahorses. 'But the Queen died and her replacement was a terrible mother who was jealous of the children and turned them into seals, only allowing them one day on land per year. When they grew older, Roderick MacCodrum, roaming the shores, found a beautiful sealskin from one of the daughters and took it back to his house. The selkie followed him and he hid her skin and asked her to be his wife. She agreed, despairing of ever returning to her now beloved ocean.'

Camilla pauses for a sip of red wine. 'Her children grew up loving the sea and singing into seashells. One day, he was out a long time and a huge wind blew against the house, dislodging the sealskin box. Out flopped her skin and she bade farewell to her children and returned to the sea. Roderick was warned to go back when a hare crossed his path on his way to work, but he never took notice. He returned later that night to find the children weeping and his selkie gone forever. He never recovered, and it's said that the sons of Roderick MacCodrum, and their offspring too, never lifted an oar to a seal thereafter. They became known as Clan MacCodrum of the Seals, a sect of the Clan Donald in the Outer Hebrides.'

'Are they still around?' asks DK.

'According to my grandmother, you need to look closely at all the Donald clan as well as the Mac-Codrums. She says the selkie still swims in their blood. Even the girls are tall and dark and speak like men with bodies as strong as any seal you are likely to see.'

Cowrie looks over to the picture of Morrigan on the mantlepiece above the fire. Her once-long, dark hair hangs over her face, her body drapes down over the chair like a seal, her tail fins close together on the floor. 'Did any of them come to Orkney?' she asks.

'Likely as not, if you believe in these myths,' explains Camilla. 'Personally, I think they make great fireside stories, but I don't believe a speck of it myself.' She hands the tototoko, a carved talkingstick Cowrie had brought with her from Aotearoa, over to Sasha, who responds with another seal story from her Inuit tradition. Cowrie follows with the tale of the tsunami and

Laukiamanuikahiki saving the small village hut and mural of Punalu'u Beach as it once was, with women shelling coconuts on the black sands and chiefs waving off a canoe to distant shores, maybe those of Aotearoa.

They share food and talkstory late into the night, then retire to their beds, contented but exhausted. Cowrie notices smoke still smouldering from the chimney in the shed and she sends out all the healing energy she can muster to Morrigan and her seal, while settling in beside Sasha, glad she is warm and safe with this dolphin woman from the north.

[28]

Morrigan wakes with a start. Beside her, the seal is breathing heavily, snorting every few minutes, and now refuses even the fresh fish that Morrigan made Squiddy bring by while the girls were over at the broch. She's sure that Cowrie, at least, has guessed what she is up to but she is almost beyond caring now. She can barely open her eyes and the exhaustion of several nights without sleep has taken over and made her feel dizzy and spacy. Maybe the fight to keep life at all costs, bring back the dead into the land of the living, is not what nature intended. Maybe this one is meant to die?

She looks down at the seal and his eyes look up to her but it is clear that he can barely register. There is a dullness behind the pupils, a lack of recognition and energy to live. Maybe he wants to die after all? Maybe I am prolonging his life unnecessarily? Perhaps he wanted to get caught? He's a wiley old bugger and would not easily fall into a fishermen's net. He knows this trap too well to be fooled. Maybe he came back to make me promise to look after his daughter, our daughter, and to see me for one last time.

The thoughts swirl about Morrigan's mind like seaweed in a storm, catching onto every small bit of debris, lurching to and fro as the swell drags them out and in again. She drifts into a fitful sleep and the seal twitches beside her then lies still.

'It's time to let go, Morrigan,' the women say. 'He'll not come back. You've had the chance to talk again and make peace. But now you must let go.' The words stream out from the walls of Skara Brae and across the sea and rocks, are flown on the wind, up and over the fields to the humble shed where Morrigan lies cuddled into the seal, trying to keep it warm and alive. She huddles closer to the mammal, folding her arms fully around the creature, even then not reaching the width of its girth. Just under the skin she smells the lobsters and crabs, the mackerels and halibut, the kelp and tangle the seal has eaten. Despite stoking the fire continually, it is still cold and she reaches for the oilskin to cover them both.

'Hold on, my love, hold on, for it is not time yet.' Morrigan pleads with the seal's destiny, but fate has already made her decision. Bit by bit, the seal shivers and trembles, each time getting weaker and weaker, then finally sleeps. It is only in this moment of peace that Morrigan has the courage to let go. 'Farewell, my love. I will see thee on t'other side again. Thank you for these last final days together.' She weeps into the soft fur of the seal, grieving more than when he first left her to go to sea. The seal dies peacefully in Morrigan's arms and she lies with him for the first few hours of sleep she has had in a week. She then rises before dawn, makes a cross from two pieces of driftwood tied together with flax, takes the shovel from the shed and starts digging.

From the cottage, Cowrie, waking for a glass of water after all the wine, glances out the window. The smoke from the shed is barely visible. But there is a figure, probably Morrigan, out in the field digging. Could this be the end? She watches as the earth and stones fly through the air and finally Morrigan slumps over the shovel. Cowrie fights the urge to go and help her. Sasha was adamant that they should leave her to her grieving. But it is hard to do so when you feel the hurt deeply inside. Maybe she'll wander on down in the morning and see if Morrigan is okay. Act casual, like she's just interested in who might be at the shed and buzz off if it feels uncomfortable and she senses Morrigan needs to be alone. Cowrie sighs, drinks the last of the water and joins Sasha in bed.

Morrigan walks to the shed and drags the dead seal on the tarpaulin he'd lain on while being removed from the boat. She gently rolls him into the grave and then lays a ring on top of his body, clutched in his fins. It is the ring that Kelpie gave her. She then plants the driftwood cross at his head. She walks back solemnly to the shed, picking up her coat, turning her back on the bay, and slowly starts up the track through the heather to her cottage.

[29]

Chop, chop, chop! The knife crashes through the Golden Wonder potatoes at an alarming rate as they are diced into squares and thrown into a huge pot on the coal range. Next under the axe are a pile of yellow turnips wincing at the fate of the tatties, then the painful process of peeling onions begins. Morrigan is glad of the excuse to cry salt tears onto the sliced and diced onions. She slides them into the pot with the blade, adds boiling water to cover and sets to cleaning the coal range and collecting more fuel for the fire from the large pile of coals in the box beside the kitchen. She attacks the huge beast of a stove with vigour, using a fork to get into the cracks, and scraping the top around the simmering pot. The smell of turnips and tatties permeates through the house, out the window and into the nearby cottages.

Cowrie wakes, sniffing the air. A strange and appealing odour of cooking vegetables greets her constantly-alert nose. She sneaks out of bed and clambers into the clothes lying on the Orkney auction chair they'd picked up for two quid. She smiles, recalling the vigorous bids for antiques and the easy pickings of everyday items. As she passes the herb garden, she picks a few chives. By the time she reaches the kitchen, Morrigan is mashing the soft turnips and tatties with milk and butter, and chucking in generous quantities of salt and pepper.

'Want a few chives to go with that?' Cowrie asks, casually.

'How did yee know they came next?' she grunts, a bit startled anybody else would be awake at this hour.

'Clapshot, right?' Cowrie grins as Morrigan nods.

'Read about it in George Mackay Brown's work. Besides, we had some soon after arriving.'

'What makes you think you'd get any?' replies Morrigan, deadpan.

'I reckoned it was to share by the size of the pot.'

'You able to see pot size through stone walls, then, Kiwi?'

This is the first time Morrigan has used the national nickname and Cowrie takes it as a small token of affection in Morrigan's own unique language of nods and grunts and half-disguised insults. 'Na. Was the smell that woke me up and called me in. Then my stomach smiled to see the size of the pot.'

Morrigan has just the edge of a grin on her face. 'Aye, it's aboot time you wrapped yer molars around some good Orkney clapshot, girlie.' She deftly piles the hot clapshot onto a plate so it is steaming and adds a huge dollop of Orkney butter on the top, which melts and slides down the large mound, resembling the Brough of Birsay, like warm, golden snow. The stains from her tears have dried on her face, which is grimy from her week long vigil in the shed. Morrigan lays two plates and two forks on the table and places the mountain of clapshot in the middle. Steam issues from it like hot lava and the flow from Kilauea crater seeping toward the ocean fills Cowrie with a longing to be back in the welcoming warmth of the Pacific. She digs into the clapshot, filling herself with its hot, comforting sweet savoury tastes. 'Like our Orkney clapshot then aye, lassie?' asks Morrigan, her mouth full.

'Sure do,' replies Cowrie, mumbling through the tatties and turnips. She finishes her mouth full. 'So how's the fishing been this week?'

Morrigan looks up, knowing from Cowrie's face that

she is aware she has not been fishing and she has probably seen her at the shed. 'Not so good. Got a damned seal in the net then had to look after him.'

'Did he survive?' asks Cowrie, almost afraid to hear the answer.

'No, lassie. They seldom do. Even the strong ones.' Morrigan concentrates hard on eating until the next helping of clapshot and gives the clear impression she does not want to talk further about it. 'So how was your week? Hope you ferryloopers didn't smash up my van.' She reaches for more salt and sprinkles it liberally over the clapshot.

'Just a few minor dents,' grins Cowrie, 'nothing too bad.'

For a moment Morrigan nearly takes the bait, then realises she is being set up. 'Yee'll be baiting lobster creels, a day for every dent, lassie,' blurts Morrigan, a slight grin betraying her.

'I'd love it,' replies Cowrie, quick as a shot. 'And the lobsters at the end.' She helps herself to another pile of clapshot. 'Wouldn't mind going fishing with ya sometime, actually. I'm a keen fisher at home. Mostly kahawai trawling from my kayak, schnapper, mullet, the odd kingfish if ya lucky.'

Morrigan shows interest for the first time since they sat down. 'Kaha-why, what the hell's that?'

'About the size of a good haddock but with dark flesh, almost red in places when smoked and brown with creamy flesh. Luscious smoked over wet manuka.'

'Manuka? Some kind of peat?' Morrigan wipes her tongue around her lips to savour the clapshot.

'Nup. It's a native. You might know it as tea tree. Good for making a fresh brew after it's steeped a few days, but it's best for smoking kahawai, any fish really.'

Cowrie reaches for the pepper to spice her remaining bites of the delicious Orkney dish.

'How's it smoked then? You hang it up in a shed and smoke it a few days or what?'

Morrigan and Cowrie enter deep into a conversation about the differences between Orcadian and Aotearoan fish-smoking practices, enjoying the familiar ones and learning from the new tips. For a half-an-hour, Morrigan relaxes and her ordeal of the past week slides gently into the deeper recesses of her heart. She loves fishing and this is the first time she and Cowrie have had a chance to have a true heart-to-heart on the things that matter in life. She's relieved the kiwi does not ask any more questions about the past week. Wise to put it behind her now. It lays to rest a whole unfinished saga from the past and maybe it's better left that way; in the past. Except for her promise to Kelpie. Morrigan yawns widely.

'I'm sorry, Morrigan. You've had a helluva week. You must be exhausted. Why don't I do the dishes and you take yourself off to bed?' Cowrie starts collecting the plates.

Morrigan stretches, yawning again. 'Best idea you've had all day.' She lifts herself wearily from the old wooden chair leaving mud stains on the straw bottom, and pushes it back into its place beside the table. Cowrie clears the remains of their dawn feast. From the doorway, Morrigan whispers gently, so as not to wake Camilla, 'Thanks, Turtle,' and exits to her bedroom.

Cowrie is left stunned. She had no idea Morrigan even knew of her nickname nor of the story behind it. And she seldom uses intimate language like this. Maybe it is a sign of some kind of acceptance? After all, they got along well at the Edinburgh Festival, though Morrigan was almost a different person then, parading under the name of Ellen and much more out-going than here in Orkney. Strange she has these names. There's still something about Morrigan Cowrie cannot quite fathom. She boils the water for the dishes and stacks the dinner plates first, tea cups next and then the large pot.

From the kitchen window, she sees the driftwood cross marking the seal's grave down the field by the shed. Beyond, the wind and sea sculpt new shapes into the rocky ledges and sandstone cliffs at the entrance to the Bay of Skaill. There is a moaning from the kelpy waters midway into the bay as the Skaill seals mourn the passing of their kin. The wailing resounds over the bay and is drawn up the fields by the inshore winds that batter the coast constantly. Morrigan hears it from her bed and a tear falls from her one open eye as she pulls the covers over her head and burrows deep into the blankets.

[30]

He lies still, as still as can be. The ferny fronds fall down over his face and around his body, touching his sides and making him ticklish. It circles around and over him, looking from side to side with its swivelling eyes, hungry and angry. Oblivious to the danger, a pair of sea horses cling tentatively to their weedy home and entwine their bodies affectionately around each other. Sandy knows the shark is after him. He watched from a distance while Fiona tried to distract him with the ink-shooting squid. That was a brave and very foolish move, but he was grateful for the time to dive down into the kelp bed they'd explored earlier, playing together.

The shark moves closer every time he circles the bed of kelp. It is only a matter of time before he sees the seal and makes his attack. Sandy is still not sure if Fiona made it back safely to her ledge. Last he saw was a cloud of blue-black ink and the shark chasing Fiona at high speed, angry and flicking its tail rapidly. But there was no blood and none of the usual play that goes with the kill, so he took that as a sign that she had made it. He has no idea what he'd do without Fe now. They have bonded for life and it is hard to find other selkies with experience of the earthly Nofin existence, who will understand what choices they have made and why, and who do not long to return to the sandy shores to see what may lie in wait for them should they lose their skins to humans again. It is a fate neither he nor Fiona now want. They have made up their minds to stay and neither has any desire to return to a human existence now.

Above him, the smell of blood lingers on the shark's

jaws as he begins to nose the kelp, looking for his prey. He knows the seal is down there somewhere and it is a waiting game to see who will give way first. The shark has plenty of time to cruise but he is hungry and eager for the sweet taste of sealmeat now. His probings get closer and closer, each time dislodging a few seahorses or scattering some mackerel feeding on the seaweed.

Fiona lies hunched in the rocky ledge, her tail being nibbled by annoying shrimps who know she cannot turn in this space to flick them off with her fore-fin. They are eating the luscious algae creatures that attach themselves to passing mammals and go along for the ride. She has edged in as far as she can to the small elongated cave, just large enough for her body. She has not dared to move since the great white launched himself at her and she was deeply grateful the rock oysters took the brunt of the blow, wounding him on the jaw. She will have given Sandy time to hide, but where and for how long?

The squid float near the surface sunning themselves in the light and glad big jaws is obsessed with the seal hiding among the kelp. It was enough to be used as potential fodder, so they'd squirt their ink at the shark, but the further indignity of having to endure a pursuit, knowing he'd catch at least two or three of them on the run, would not be their idea of a good day. They watch, idly, as the shark noses in amongst the bladderwrack, edging nearer and nearer to the seal. Suddenly, there is a fast lunge and the seaweed swirls with motion, a tussle which sends feeding flat fish and saithe rushing out in all directions and seahorses floating from their weedy branches. This is no play but a fight to the death, as the tail of the great white swings back and forth while its jaws cling on and crunch into flesh. All they can see is the shark tail and lower body flinging itself around above the kelp while the jaws lunge at their prey.

Blood seeps out from the seaweed, swirling along and past the ledge Fiona hides under and her whole being freezes. She heard the lunge and realised Sandy was hiding amongst the kelp they swam through recently, so playfully then. Her fins beat helplessly against the rocky cave which feels more like a grave to her now. Will the shark take a bite and then swim away or will he be in for the kill today? More blood seeps past and she burrows her head deeper into the cave, unable to witness the scene to come when the shark will swim with Sandy to the surface of the water and fling him up in the air, taking pleasure in the crash as he hits the water and watching him weaken and weaken, biting his jaws into the flesh again and again until he is limp and not able to struggle any longer. Then he will eat seal flesh, every last scrap, with only a few morsels floating down past her for smaller fish to munch. If she had diverted the shark and taken the attack, she could at least have saved her Sandy.

More scuffling, then in the distance she sees the shark swimming away, its prey lodged within its large jaws. She turns back into the dark pit of the cave, never wanting to swim out again.

[31]

A white dove hovers in mid-air, above two seraphim and cherubim. St Francis of Assisi and St Catherine of Siena shine out from their painted stained glass shrines. In the centre, above the altar, a madonna with child. Golden curtains embrace the sanctuary and the altar is flanked by exquisite candelabra. The semi-rounded shape of the chapel embraces them, makes them feel as if back in the womb. Hard to believe that the sanctuary gold curtains were paid for by prisoners of war, that the tabernacle wood came from a wrecked sailing ship, the stained glass windows are painted onto board over corrugated iron and the beautiful altar, rail and holy water stoop are all created from concrete.

There is such a holy feeling as they stand in the Italian Chapel, built from two corrugated iron Nissen huts by prisoners of war on the island of Lambholm. They cannot keep back the tears. It is difficult to take in that they are now standing on the site of Camp 60 which housed several hundred Italian prisoners near the end of the Second World War in Orkney. The men were sent to construct the Churchill Barriers, a series of ugly concrete causeways designed to seal the eastern approaches to Scapa Flow where the British navy was housed during the war. Amidst the squalor and depression and point-lessness of war, the Italians transformed the huts of thirteen camps by making pathways, planting gardens with vibrant flowers, building a theatre with props and scenery and a recreation hut. Then, under the guidance of an inspired artist, Domenico Chioccetti, they began work on the chapel in 1943.

'This is the first time I have stood inside a church and actually felt it was sacred,' admits Monique, deeply touched by the experience. She runs her hand along the intricately carved wrought iron sanctuary screen and looks up to the most lovingly painted Madonna with child she has ever seen. 'I wish my father could have seen this. His only memories of this decade are the scars his body still bears from being forcibly sterilised.' Tears run down her cheeks as she looks longingly at the Madonna looking longingly at her child.

Camilla touches her shoulder gently. 'It is beautiful.' She genuflects before the altar and crosses herself.

DK reads from the Chapel Preservation Committee's guidebook that the two Nissen huts were placed end-to-end and joined together, initially as both a school and a church, but once Chioccetti began work on the altar, the chapel had to be painted also and they used the entire space so all the prisoners could worship. Ideas flamed through the artist's mind as he continued work, enlisting many other prisoners to help.

'He only had recycled rubbish and scrap material to work from, and to create such an exquisite work of art from what others consider rubbish is what I find so inspirational.' Cowrie is close to tears herself as she admires the beautiful stonework and carved stone latticework which is painted onto curved board laid over the corrugated iron.

'Get this,' exclaims DK. 'You know that amazing statue of St George slaying the dragon which I liked so much at the entrance. The prisoners made that from barbed wire covered in concrete. Imagine sculpting something so intricate from that.'

Cowrie glances out the window at the impressive statue, the Italian flag flying proudly to the right of it.

The barbed wire brings back painful memories of deep cuts and gashes in her skin when they climbed the barriers of army-laid barbed wire to protest apartheid in South Africa. They had forced a racist tour to end and helped a regime to topple. A generation of kiwis wore the marks of barbed wire cuts on their arms and legs and bodies from that period. But to turn the image around, use it for an awesome work of art, is a truly radical act.

DK informs them that after the war, the South European arm of the BBC broadcast a programme on the chapel in the summer of 'fifty-nine, including a conversation with Chioccetti who had been traced to Moena, a small village in the Dolomites. The *Orkney Herald* had subsequently run a series of articles re-awakening interest in the chapel and the story of its construction and people flocked in from all over Orkney and further afield to see it. Local Orcadians brought Chioccetti back to the chapel in 1960, and he later did restoration work on it, and thus began a long and wonderful relationship between Chioccetti's family, the village of Moena and Orkney. Some of the prisoners who worked on the chapel were also brought back for a service to honour their work in 1992.

'To conceive of such a work of creation amidst the destruction of war blows my mind.' Uretsete stands in awe of the curved structure above her head holding the most moving frescoes she has ever seen.

DK reads that when the prisoners came back to see the chapel again in 1992 they were moved to tears and one, Bruno Volpi, said, 'People cannot be judged by their precarious situations. Their culture, spirit and will to express themselves in creative thoughts and deeds are stronger than any limitation to freedom. This is the spirit that gave birth to the works of art on Lambholm.'

'That says it all.' A tear slides down Monique's cheek.

At the Ring of Brodgar at dawn, they could not imagine any man-made structure that could equal this combination of creative effort working alongside nature but, they agree, the chapel, set amidst a field of sheep grazing among the rocks and wildflowers and looking out over the dazzling waters of Scapa Flow, could be a contender. They walk about, sit, meditate and enjoy the atmosphere, finding it inspiring to know that such an act of pure spirit could be created amidst the destructiveness of war. What courage it took these prisoners to negotiate for the necessities to enact their vision and what flexibility on the part of their captors.

'If Skara Brae showed no archeological evidence of the inhabitants having any weapons at all in the Stone Age, then this is our twentieth century contribution to peace. Long may it be preserved.' As they wend their way reluctantly from the sanctuary of the chapel, Monique drops coins into the preservation box and the others follow suit.

'If we cannot get permission to perform talkstory at the Ring of Brodgar, then I would opt for this as a possibility,' suggests Uretsete.

'It's been used for performances during the St Magnus Festival, the most recent in 1999 when Maria Chioccetti returned for services at the chapel after Domenico died, and it is dedicated to the people of Orkney and all visitors, so it may be possible.' Camilla has noted this as next on her list after Brodgar. She's already made contact with a local farmer who will let them use the land nearest Brodgar for their festival.

They drive over the historic Churchill Barriers to South Ronaldsey and begin a tour of the artists' galleries on the island. A wild, stone-clad beach just before the

145

rise to the Hoxa Tapestry Gallery offers an appealing place for lunch and they spread their smoked haddock, Swanney cheese, fresh Argos bread, Orkney butter and tomatoes, peppers, shallots, chives and Sasha's blue cheese dip in containers and boxes onto the old tartan blanket they'd found in the van and tuck into a delicious feast. Cowrie wishes there had been some clapshot to smear over the bread as well, but all the others know of this dawn feast is the absence of a few tatties from the huge sack they'd bought from an Orkney potato farmer.

The sun sparks dazzling silver lights from the calm blue sea, tinged with aqua as it curves around the bay. Red, yellow, brown and cream sandstone rocks carpet the beach, with a sandy edge near the water. Many of the rocks have been sculpted by the sea and feature scenes as wild as the imagination likes to conjure. The swirling designs, often raised above the surface of the rocks, show dragons with fiery smoke and tails trailing under the rock, dolphins leaping from the waves, whales floating on the surface, lizards and geckoes creeping along the brown slits, a turtle with a piece of kelp in its mouth, a seal frolicking in the deep, another lying in a rocky crevice.

They comb the beach collecting rocks and shells that appeal to them, driftwood for art work and the fire, old discarded fishermen's nets, useful for the garden they are planning as a surprise for Morrigan, and also find a perfect fish skeleton which DK adds to her collection. The Orkney beaches offer so much and they are inspired by the work of the prisoners during such devastation in Europe, that they agree they will never bemoan the lack of materials or inspiration again.

'Hey, let's do a beach storytelling workshop, where stones and rocks and shells and found objects are used as a starting point for stories from the participants.' The idea takes off like wildfire, and they begin the process now, each one bringing a new perspective to the beachy artefacts, coaxing them to life with memory and imagination. After talkstory and beachcombing, they make their way back over the dunes to the car and continue up the hill to the Hoxa Tapestry Gallery.

'I find tapestries as boring as knitting,' admits DK and opts to walk the surrounding cliffs with impressive views out over Scapa Flow.

Monique eyes some ruined stone houses with grass growing into the turf on their roofs, and a few black-and-white cows munching in the field next door, while the sea startles with its deep blue under the rare Orkney sun. 'I'll check out those ruins.'

The others walk into the gallery and are stunned by the combination of poetry and visuals, with the tapestries often weaving words around the edges or inspired by poetry. The artist has made cards of the woven magic and the work embraces a wonderful mixture of everyday life and inspired universal themes. Cowrie moves slowly around the tapestries, noting the different stitchwork, and admiring one where the artist walked down to the beach at night and focused on the moon's trail over the water and up the sand. She turned around and then saw it connected with her shadow moving out behind her, as if she were also a moon casting a glow over the land. According to the notes, she then walked back to sketch the idea and began work on the tapestry soon after.

There are two women deeply involved in discussing the patterns and each tapestry draws another story from them. Cowrie turns to face the final wall and is knocked out by the design. Here lies her recurring dream of selkies, flowing in and out of the water, with flutes, violins, calling to the sea and the land, acting as a bridge between two worlds. One selkie has hair flowing from her head like seaweed and into the landscape, forming the clouds above the scene.

It is a commissioned work and different from all the others. It leaps out at you from the wall and takes you into a deep dreamspace where the lines between reality and fantasy are blurred, where the separations between human and animal are no longer relevant, where the seascape blends into the landscape and the borders between land and sea and sky merge.

Her knees weaken and she has to sit down. She feels her legs turning into fins, her fins flowing through the sea, her body moving along a bed of kelp. It touches her undersides and runs along her belly to the tip of her tail. Above her, squid dance in the sunlight, playing with the patterns it casts on the water. Below her, a seal seems caught in the kelp. She dives toward it to help. A shadow is cast over her body, moving like a cloud over the sea. She looks up to see a great white shark swimming over her head, circling and returning. She ducks into the seaweed, hoping her fins will pull her fast enough to escape. She hovers amongst the swirling branches, and looks up to see giant jaws coming towards her through the kelp. It is aiming for the seal trapped below her but she is caught between them.

[32]

Layered sandstone crags rise up from the swirling waters like tufa from Lake Mono, each with its own design and story. A castle tower in one, a surfing dolphin in the next. The sea splashes up the sides of the rocks, each time trying to reach higher on the incoming tide. A pink thrift pokes a tufted head out from the cliff edges and fulmars nest in the rock ledges below. Ahead, an ancient fisherman's hut, made of dry stone walls and flagstone roof, now covered in turf and sprouting a thick head of sea-green grass, hides among the wildflowers, sunk into the cliff and looking out over a rocky bay. Up the sides of the banks leading from the bay, the shapes of fishing boats, their prows rested in the sandy loam, are etched into the hills. You can see them now, braced by the rocks below, proudly waiting for the dawn and their launching into the wild seas off the Skipi Geo near the Brough of Birsay.

They clamber down to the beach being careful not to disturb the nesting fulmars on the rocks beside and above them. The geo forms a sheltered bay with huge layered rock stacks either side and a naturally sloping beach of rounded pebbles and sculpted rocks. Rusty remains of an old winch, used to draw the boats up the beach, lie about and between the rocks with old bones and limpet shells, their flesh once used for bait. The nousts where the boats once lay make it easy to imagine a bustling community of fishers, each helping the others with their boats, setting off for the day's fishing, and returning to winch up their dories, clean the day's catch, set it up to dry or smoke, then retiring to their stone cottage to down a mug of home-brewed whisky. For so many fishers, estimated up to sixty at a time, to share a bay so small, they must have created a communal working system, much of which survives today on the islands.

'Check this out!' DK holds up the skeleton of a bird's head, possibly an oystercatcher, which has aged with time and been stained a deep brown by the tangle flown in on the waves and drying on the rocks.

'Ooo. How revolting.' Camilla turns her face away. 'How can you touch that thing, DK? Don't you know that germs live in old skulls and even on feathers. You should not touch them with your bare hands.'

DK grimaces and holds the bone skeleton close to her face, nose-to-nose and pretends to tongue the beak. 'But look, Camilla. She's such a sweet creature. Look at her beak. I could kiss her.' DK does exactly that and Camilla turns away and walks back from the surf towards the safety of the cliffs. DK grins, delighted to get such a strong reaction from her. She enjoys baiting Camilla, sees why so many English escaped to the wildness of Scotland or Orkney or America or New Zealand in search of freedom from such a rule-bound civilisation, so disconnected from nature, in life and in death. What could be more beautiful, reasons DK, than the shapes of this bird's head and the textures of the action of sea and tangle in colouring its skull, a work of art created by nature and thus honouring this creature after her death.

Uretsete throws her a glance, as if warning her not to upset Camilla any more and then distracts her by scrambling over the pebbles with some interesting shells she has found. Among the limpets, ranging from cream to dark brown, are bright yellow shells that look like they might have been used by hermit crabs for a home, and two beautiful crab carcasses, one in varying shades of green and one whose back holds red and ochre designs, with some moss-like greenery around its eye sockets. DK is immediately attracted to the crab shells and holds them up to the sun to see the patterns through their sea-washed and now thin structures. In the centre of the green crab lies a heart with rays of sun shooting out from its orb. She nudges Uretsete. 'Is this our shell, then?' and throws her a charming grin. Uretsete nuzzles into DK's shoulder and smiles. Above them, the fulmars, who nest for life, squawk in affirmation. One leaves the nest and swoops around them, skimming the tops of the waves then returning to its mate, with a fishy surprise in its beak. Uretsete and DK admire the grace of its flight, and its agility in landing back on the small rocky ledge, less than a foot wide, that serves as their home in the cliff-face.

Above them, Sasha and Cowrie continue walking along the cliff-edge out to the end of the Point of Nether Queena. Facing the sea, the giant wing-span of a whale in flight, as if its flukes are suspended in mid-air, grows out from tufts of soft pink thrift and stems of wavy sea-green grass. Beyond, rocks lead out into the wild Atlantic Ocean. They lie under the gigantic whalebone in a hollow carved into the grass, and look up at its cracked surfaces, covered in yellow lichen, and its mysterious wing-like form. 'What part of the whale do you reckon this is?' asks Cowrie.

'It's the first vertebrae, or atlas bone,' explains Sasha, admiring the shape as it stretches out and down like a bird in mid-flight. 'But what I am wondering is how it got here.'

'Ah, I can tell you that,' replies Cowrie, 'since I read about it in DK's guidebook. It was washed into the bay at Doonagua Geo over a hundred years ago now, then found and mounted onto a rib bone and placed here, looking out to sea.'

'Almost like a guardian of the cliffs?'

'Exactly. I reckon it protects the coasters. So many fishermen were lost at sea in Orkney. I noticed this visiting the graveyard in Finstown one day when Morrigan was repairing her lobster pots.'

'She seems to be recovering from the death of the seal.'

'I'm not so sure. She has her good days and her off days. But I've seen her more than once bending over the grave site in the dawn hours when I get up for a pee and she returns from her fishing.'

'You mean she buried the seal somewhere near us?'

'Sure did. Down by the farm shed. She even made a driftwood cross for the grave.'

'How do you know?'

Cowrie blushes. 'I saw her burying the seal. My Woolworth's bladder had me up again in the dawn. I watched her digging the grave.'

'Why didn't you go and help her?'

'I remembered what you said about leaving her to her own devices and felt she needed time alone to grieve.'

'Sounds like you're talking about her burying her lover and not a seal,' laughs Sasha.

'What if they were one and the same?' asks Cowrie, amazed she has voiced the suspicion that had been swimming through her subconscious for days.

'If it was a selkie then it would have changed form once it was out of the water and back on dry land,' Sasha notices the whale-bone, its shape suggesting flight, as if it might dive, bird-like, back into the sea.

'Not necessarily. What if it was so wounded it could not muster the strength to shed its skin?'

'Possible, maybe. You really want to solve this mystery, eh Turtle?'

'What d'ya mean? Of course I do.'

'Just that some mysteries are best left alone. Watch your finscape, Turtle. You may find out more than you want to know.' Sasha twines her fingers around Cowrie's and pulls her close. 'Besides, I have other plans for you.' She kisses Cowrie gently on the cheek, working her way to her ears and back down her neck. Her hot breathe excites Cowrie, and her nipples harden beneath her shirt. She responds, running her tongue over Sasha's lips, tenderly vibrating the lower then upper lip until Sasha is wet with desire, then slowly entering the inside of her mouth which opens up to her like a rainbow cave, showered with sunlight through its moist wet walls. Their tongues play, dancing on the surge of their tides, swirling with the ebb and flow, surfing onto the wet rocks of their teeth and sliding under their swelling tongued waves, rising and falling with the flow. Their bodies entwined in the grassy hollow, they follow their instinctual desires, urged on by an oystercatcher with nothing better to do than watch as she waits for the tide to turn, revealing tasty morsels for her lunch.

By the time the others reach them, Cowrie and Sasha are sitting under the arched wings of the ancient whalebone, looking as if they are about to soar out into the wild ocean beyond, their arms entwined around the back of the bone, their bodies leaning against its strong embrace. The deep blue Atlantic beckons them and one by one, DK, Uretsete, Monique and Camilla perch on the cliff edge, their legs dangling over, while the oyster-catchers screech warnings not to come nearer to their nesting young, hidden among the rocks strewn below. Beside them, the sea washes up the layered ledges surrounding the geo, one large structure looking like the 'Titanic', listing on its side, the waves licking its once magnificent interior, its carcass now used as a home for fulmars.

Spoots spring forward in thrusty jumps and land in crevices beneath a mound of Orkney oysters and between the rows of live scallops, lapping up the salt water stream that bursts out above their heads in the live seafood pools at Finstown. Women walk about in large yellow rubber boots, plunging into the ponds with nets to scrape up a dozen scallops for this or that restaurant or local fish shop and packing them into polythene bags within boxes, ready to be driven to their destination within minutes. Morrigan stands watching the spoots, behaving as if they are still in the sea. She leans against the doorway and nods to one of the workers who comes over. 'Is Shelley aboot?' she asks, dangling her pipe from her mouth.

'Aye. Loading the truck.' The woman yells at the top of her voice. 'Shelley. There's a fisher come to see yer.'

Shelley replies that she'll be there in a tick and Morrigan thanks the woman and turns toward the sea. A few dories bob up and down on the tide and most of the fishers are back from their night raids of the ocean, with a few late risers still sailing toward Finstown in the distance. A couple of sheldros poke their red bills into the sand, their black-and-white feathers ruffled by the wind and their pinky-red feet covered in mud and traces of tangle. Nearby, one of the fishers is repairing his cottage which is among a line of similar ones right on the seashore, and he braces himself against the wind as he stands on the roof, spreading tar with a tall mop. Some of the tar runs down the slope and drops off in gluggy splashes onto the flowers below and his missus runs out of the house and scolds him for being so careless. The fisher just grins, unable to be seen by her, and continues his tarring.

'What are you doing here?' asks a voice from behind.

Morrigan swings around and catches the look of annoyance in Shelley's beautiful sea-green eyes. 'I'm sorry to bother you Shelley, but there's some news I need to tell you. Can we meet for lunch at the inn?'

Shelley shrugs her shoulders. 'I'm busy today. Got two lorries to load and a heap of orders. Maybe tomorrow.'

Morrigan looks concerned. 'If you wish. But I think we should talk as soon as possible.'

'If it's more of this selkie gossip, then I don't want to hear it.'

Morrigan blushes. 'Not exactly. But I think you need to know. It's high time a few things were explained and I ken your father would have wanted this.'

Shelley notices another spoot on the run and swoops down to grab it with her net. 'This one's not getting away.' She picks it up in her hand, and throws it toward Morrigan. 'Here, this'll do for your breakfast.'

The spoot, sensing it is now out of its natural watery home, sends a spout of water into Morrigan's face. She recoils and throws the spoot back into the sea water. 'Save it for the orders.' Morrigan begins walking away then calls back over her shoulder, 'See you at the inn at twelve and thirty tomorrow.'

Shelley yells back 'maybe', and plunges her net into the water after the spoot, catching it as it is about to shoot under the oysters. 'Gotcha, young laddie. Good work!' She lets it go, thanking the spoot for doing what she has wanted to do for years, spit in Morrigan's face. Shelley blames Morrigan for the bad tension between her parents and knew the gossip about Morrigan having an affair with her father. She saw them several times leaning on the sea wall, fixing nets together, and once kissing in the alley. She wanted to tell her mother but feared it would mean the end and shut her mouth against all the gossips, helping her mother build a wall around them. After her father was lost at sea, and all the selkie stories began, she blamed Morrigan for taking her father away, coaxing him from his home.

In fact, the huge geo that had formed in the rift between her father and mother had begun long before Morrigan was on the scene. One night, she recalled an argument that began in the kitchen while her father was filleting the haddock. Her mother came in and complained about the smell and asked why he didn't do it outside like the other fishers. He replied it was too bloody cold out there and in any case this was his house too. She said it was hers and not his ever since he'd been seeing that fisher-hussy, and if push came to shove, then she would fight for it in a law court and news of their affair would be broadcast about Finstown and all over Orkney. He seemed shocked she knew and he begged her forgiveness, saying he'd never do it again. But he did, because just days later, Shelley saw him kissing Morrigan behind the fishing cottages. Another time, they were humping on a blue dory, upturned against the wind and rain. She recalled their bare bums floating through the air in an almost hypnotic movement and being entranced and horrified at once.

She ran away and refused to come home for two days. The old stone barn on the hill had provided her a welcome refuge. She wailed and wailed, knowing the end would be in sight and one day her mother would just walk out or order him away. But just three days later, he did not return from fishing and his dory was later found drifting alone, his lobster pots still intact. It was as if he'd jumped into the sea and left them floating. She saw the boat after it was recovered. It had not overturned nor lost its catch. Dead lobsters were strewn about the boxes on the floor of the boat and birds had tried to peck at them through the holes in the creels. It was creepy. And it was all Morrigan's fault.

Since then, Morrigan had tried to befriend her, especially after her mother was lost at sea. Maybe it was her guilty conscience, but Shelley would not have a bar of it. Morrigan always came to her school or later her workplace so she had to be reasonably polite. Once she had gone to the inn to talk with her, but afterwards she felt angry, wished she'd yelled at her, spat in her face as she made the spoot do. She grins, just thinking about how good that felt. Everyone always said how nice Shelley was, and how good she was. Well, she'd show them a thing or two when it came to defending her family. Too many tales had been slushed around town already. She'd remained silent through it all, but today, for the first time, she'd answered back. She felt okay about it too, but just a little guilty, since she knew Morrigan regretted her actions, otherwise she wouldn't want to be kind to her, would she?

Shelley muses over the invitation to meet, curious to know if there is any substance to Morrigan's urgency or whether it is simply another vain attempt to make friends. She brushes the seawater into a grate in the floor and decides she will make up her mind tomorrow whether to see Morrigan or not. Keep her waiting. Besides, she is looking forward to the storytelling workshop and is not sure she wants to draw herself away from that just to see Morrigan.

Morrigan ambles along the waterfront, smoking her

pipe and wondering how she will explain everything to Shelley, and if she will be given the chance to do so. How much should she tell her? Maybe it's best to let sleeping seal pups lie? She looks over to the boats tied up in the safety of the inner harbour and sees her own dory bobbing about on the tide. She recalls the day she named her. Squiddy was there and he thought it'd attract more trouble after all the stories going about town. 'Yer dinna want to call her 'Selkie Too', Morrigan. Yeel be askin for trouble,' he said. Morrigan stood back, considered his comment, then leaned forward with her brush and painted a blue border around the brown lettering, telling him it'd give them something to talk about then. But maybe Squiddy was right? Maybe she should leave well alone. She puffs on her pipe then weaves left up the road and heads towards the Pomona Inn. She knows Squiddy will be holding up the bar and onto his fifth Scapa on the rocks by now, and bleating on about the bloody Tories and what they have down to ruin the life of the workers. But he's always a good ear and reasonable company and that's just what Morrigan needs right now.

She walks into the inn and sure enough, there is Squiddy leaning on the bar. His torn sweater, with holes in the elbows, is the same old brown one he's worn for decades, ever since Morrigan has known him. He is surrounded by other fishers and his hand is raised, his finger pointing to the heavens. 'And them up there,' he says, as she draws near, 'them up there will not know the bloody difference between Tony Blair and Margaret Thatcher. Once there was a keen rift between the Tories and Labour and now their shiny boots are tarred with the same bloody feathers. How's a bloke to vote at all? Might was well stay out fishing.'

'Or swig a Scapa, eh, Squiddy,' one of the fishers says,

ordering another pint of Dark Island and making sure the barmaid pours it with a decent froth on the top.

Morrigan joins them and orders a Scapa and another for Squiddy, who looks dangerously close to finishing his glass of whisky. 'And as for those scroungy Lib Dems, I don't reckon I'd trust a slithering spoot more than their spiel,' adds Squiddy.

'Aye, but the opening of the Scottish Parliament didn't exactly fill us with pride, now did it, with all them fancy politicians filling their own coffers and claiming all sorts of expenses and upping their salaries before they'd even got mud on their boots.' Finn dashes his mug onto the counter as if to emphasise his point and orders another Dark Island.

'Give 'em a chance, laddie,' says Scotty. 'When yer've lived through the number of English botch-ups I have, and their hacking away at Scottish rights, then yer'd be pleased to have as many Scots with bums on seats as possible.'

'Too true, Scotty, at least we've got the boys back to Edinburgh. The poms stole our hearts and souls as well as our voting rights and our land in the seventeen hundreds, and we've done well to rip 'em back again, this time by legal vote. We should support those buggers fool enough to give up a good days fishin ter don a bloody uncomfortable black suit and tie and be crammed indoors all day with people screamin' at each other. Me, I'd rather wear a sealskin than be sucked into one of those skin-fitting suits. Whadya reckon, Morrigan?'

Morrigan points down to her dungarees and yellow rubber boots. 'Luckily, I have the choice, Fergy,' she replies, enigmatically. They think she means simply the choice of women's or men's clothing, and laugh.

'Buggered if I'd wear a skirt, girlie. You're welcome to

it,' replies Squiddy, knowing it is guaranteed to blow the wind up Morrigan's sails.

'All you'd need was a good Orkney gale and yer balls'd freeze off Squiddy,' grins Scottie. 'I wouldn't recommend it either.' He laughs at his own joke and the others join in. Morrigan does not deign to reply, though she thinks a bit of deballing would not hurt some of these fellas when they get too tanked up on Scapa.

Gradually, the conversation moves off smut and back onto politics, to the day's catch and back to local council politics, to re-ordering rounds and back to the laws controlling the fishers and making their lives harder by the day. Morrigan drinks with the best of them, downing at least as much in as short a time, which endows her with honorary balls in their eyes, along with her strong skills as a fisher. She's known as a hard worker and a hard drinker by them and she knows how to stand up to authority as good as any fisher born. Though she's a strange one too. Scottie watches her fill her glass like a bloke and wonders, again, if she is one of those dykes. But then, she never would've shagged Kelpie if that was true. He refills his glass and looks out the window of the inn. In the distance, young Shelley from the fishfarm is wandering along the sea wall. She's a dreamy one that lassie. Always with her head in the clouds. Never recovered from the deaths of her parents. Or maybe it was the selkie gossip afterwards. That'd be enough to kill some folks, he thinks, as he stretches his neck to down another mouth of liquid gold, then burps.

[34]

Fiona skulks in her cave, letting the shrimps eat off her back and face and belly, not caring how ticklish they are and not even finning them away. She recalls the day Sandy came to call her into the sea, how lonely she had felt among the upper class of Orkney, how she often longed to be dragged out into the ocean and never seen again. She resisted his advances at first then fell under his sealy spell, took to the water like she was born there, began a new life in her underwater world, the kind of life she dreamed of having in her earthly existence but could never attain. Her father had her life mapped ahead of her. She would marry an earl he had lined up who owned a castle in Scotland. She would be taken away from the Orkney she loved, the sea which had nourished her soul since her birth, the rocky beaches she walked along at night when the others were asleep. She would rather drown than accept that fate.

Sandy had also known loneliness. He had come from a poor family whose crofts had gradually been abandoned and left to ruin. One by one, all his family members flew Orkney to pursue their lives elsewhere. They'd sailed to many parts of the globe, from joining the Hudson Bay Company in Canada, to goldmining in Australia and fishing in New Zealand. From the far south, they talked of endless sunlight and sea and nights that closed in around nine even in the summer. At first they couldn't even sleep. The rhythms were all wrong. Then they got used to it. They talked endlessly about the weather and how warm it was. No harsh winds off the Baltic or bashing seas from the Atlantic. Few treacherous waters like the Pentland Firth to negotiate, although a few boats had sunk in Cook Strait, they said.

She once suggested to Sandy that they swim as far south as the Pacific, see what it was like for themselves, and he agreed it could be fun if they did it in stages and followed the currents to make it an easier ride. But now she would never go alone. She could barely raise the energy to swim from her cave and move out from the Bay of Skaill, let alone get to Marwick Head and the Brough of Birsay, never mind the South Pacific. The shrimps munch around her eyes and Fiona flicks her head to send them flying off in all directions, just to return and try again a few seconds later.

Around her, life goes on as normal, as if the shark had never attacked and ripped away one of their community. The seahorses sway on their ferny fronds of tangle, the mackerel play games amidst the dabberlocks, the saithe munches on tiny rock cods at the edges of her ledge. Hermit crabs clamber over the rocky ocean floor carrying their huge shell homes on their backs. A few haddock cruise by as if they own the sea. Sandy liked to bait them by telling them their brothers and sisters were fried with tatties and served up all over Scotland and Orkney in various oatmeal and crumbly batters, but the haddock would simply turn a blind eye and swim in the other direction. They would be free to pursue their dreams now Sandy is gone.

Fiona moans and rolls over, flicking the shrimps from her face. Their darting back and forward and eating from her skin annoys her and she moves so she can flick a fin and get rid of them.

But she hits something hard instead, something oily. She opens her eyes but cannot focus.

Between the rocky ledges, a vision appears. It is

Sandy, resplendent and strong, but with a battered fin still oozing blood. His eyes are so full of love, Fiona knows his spirit must still be alive somewhere. His whiskers had been brushing her face and she had tried to flick him away as if he were a shrimp. He looks amused and sways his tail to and fro, swanning away the mackerel gathering at his side to see what morsels might fall off. He skims his body along the edge of the ledge as if to urge her out of the crevice. Fiona closes her eyes. She cannot bear to feel the pain of separation from Sandy. The shrimps close in on her again. She flicks her fins and again touches solid skin. This time, Sandy yells, 'Ouch. Cut it out, Fiona! I've had enough of a scare with the great white let alone my own lover attacking me!' She opens her eyes with a start. Maybe this really is Sandy and not a vision. But how could it be?

She tentatively reaches out and touches his beautiful oily skin. He motions her to swim out of the cave. She floats out skimming the water with her tail and keeping her fins by her side to avoid scraping her skin and Sandy nudges his nose the full length of her body and up the other side until he reaches her face again. He floats with his cheek on hers, nuzzling her affectionately.

Fiona fins him delicately, lovingly, unable to speak at first. Gradually she realises it truly is Sandy and a swelling tide of relief fills her from tail to nose. 'How did yee escape the shark? I saw him swimming off with yee in his mouth.'

'It wasn't me. He chased me down into the tangle and I went deeper and deeper into the maze but he sniffed me out. Just as he went to attack, a turtle swam across banging her shell into his face. He was knocked off guard and I thought I was dreaming. Before he could regain his senses, the turtle had turned her back and smashed into his other eye. He lunged forward, but she deftly swam away and his jaws sank into the flesh of a giant octopus who swung around and wrapped all her tentacles over the shark's face. He tried to wriggle free but the octopus was hanging on for dear life. She knew if she let go he would sink his jaws back into her. Blood was streaming from her body and one of her tentacles, but she clung on as he swam away. Sometime, he'd have to drop her or she'd see her opportunity and duck into a nearby cave where he could not enter. I surfaced from the tangle to see them disappear, then stayed low until I felt there was no chance of the shark returning. I scraped my fin on the edge of an oyster bed, but it'll heal just fine. Then I began searching for yee, my love. I am so relieved to see yee safe.' He nudges Fiona gently.

'Sandy, my sweet, I love yee.' Fiona's eyes brim with tears that are soon washed away by the sea. She brushes against his fin, checking to see it really will heal.

Sandy rubs his strong fin along her belly affection-ately. 'And I yee, my love. Thank yee for distracting the shark with that ink-shooting squid. That was a brave and brilliant move, if dangerous.'

'I'd do it again if I thought yee'd come out alive. Sandy, let's swim south next year, explore new seas.'

Sandy's eyes widen. 'I'd love to, Fe, but just for one season. I have to return to Orcadian waters. I will not desert these islands as my kin did. I made a promise to meself on that.'

'Me too. I'd just like one summer of warmth while it is cold up here.'

'We both deserve it. But yee do realise that the great white haunts the New Zealand and Australian coasts too, Fe.'

Fiona looks quite shocked, then laughs. 'So long as

there are squids and octopus there too, we'll be safe, my love.'

Sandy flings his body back, does a flip and roars with laughter. 'Yee should've seen the sight of that shark swimming away with an octopus wrapped around his ugly face. I tell yee, Fe, I'll remember it to the end of me days.'

'But how come a turtle intervened? I have not seen turtles around Orcadian waters ever, though I hear they existed when Orkney was once floating below the equator, in very ancient times.' Fiona is convinced his fin will be fine and looks up into his face.

'I must admit, Fe, I have never seen a turtle here either. She must have drifted off her natural course. The odd turtle has been sighted in colder waters but usually if a storm has interrupted her journey. But they are known to swim long distances and be very resilient.'

'Well, let's hope she survives. What an act of courage,' replies Fe, beginning to munch on kelp and realising how hungry she is after this ordeal and her time in the cave.

A dark shape floats over them and for one terrible moment they think it is the shark returning. They look up to see a school of passing Manta Rays, headed for warmer waters. Their fins glide like wings through the water, their movement as graceful as angels.

[35]

Sasha rubs coconut cream tinged with gardenia oil into Cowrie's back. 'Ouch! That bit hurts!' Cowrie winces as her hand reaches the shoulder blade. She cannot recall bashing it against anything but it hurts as if she has fallen on it. Sasha works the sore area with her fingers moving deftly around the swollen patch, being careful not to irritate it further.

'I thought Turtles had hard shells and could withstand pain,' Sasha replies.

'They don't like pain at all in any way, shape or form,' mutters Cowrie, her face still buried in the pillow.

Sasha grins. 'Then Turtle shells are softer than I thought. You shouldn't go swimming into rocky ledges.'

'No rocks this time. I can't think how I bruised it so badly. Must've been when you were kissing me under the whalebone. You kayakers don't know your own strength!' Cowrie laughs.

Sasha pins her on the bed. 'Watch out, Turtle, or I might repeat the kissing to see if it can wound the other shoulder as well.' She grins and starts kissing Cowrie's neck and up around her ears and then down her back, gently tonguing her way across the shoulder blade. Cowrie moans with delight. Sasha's tongue gets hotter and hotter until she can barely lick. She runs it along the spine and returns to the wounded area. There is a heat emanating from within that is like hot lava swarming under the surface. Back at the spine, it is more like the sea swirling either side of a long rocky ledge.

Her tongue returns to the shoulder and works its way down her back, as her fingers softly run over her hips.

Cowrie moans sweetly as Sasha enters her from behind, her fingers parting the soft fur at the lip of her cave and moving tenderly along the shaft of her clitoris, until it swells and swells, like the sea moving a wave to its height. Cowrie moans into her pillow, feeling Sasha's other hand move over her hardened, rising nipples, as she gently swells the waves below.

She enters into dreamspace, as Sasha's tongue slides down her back and slithers into the cave. She is floating on an ocean swell, her shell warmed by the sun, her belly fluid, her fins outstretched. The hot lava of Pelee flows into the sea and surges towards her, entering her body and warming her insides. The rocking motion of the ocean awakes all her senses and water flows from her mouth into her belly, joining the fire midstream. Liquid tongues lap her juices and she sizzles as fire and water meet within her. She drifts in bliss, ripples entering her again and again and again, sending waves of pleasure through her body and out to the tips of her fins. The sea rocks her, rocks within her, mingling its salty water with tongues of fire. She surrenders fully to the seasurge and drifts out with the tide.

Flames of fire surf down Sasha's arm and into the cave. She floats on air, rising above the waves, flying through the waters as if in her kayak, then plunging back in again, diving to the depth of the cave and rising to surface to take air. Her whole body shakes as if an earthquake has erupted through the water, sending hot lava streaming through her veins. She reaches for the tip of the mountain, strokes gently, as it rises and rises, then explodes. Her dolphin tail surges through the water, powering her into the air, and she flies above, skimming the tops of the waves with her belly, finning, finning, finning her way to freedom. She rides the surf like a dolphin in flight, soaring at the top of the wave, surging down into its belly, to rise on the next wave, and surf its crest to the curve of its concave body, in tune with its motion, as one with the sea, with Cowrie.

A shaft of sun shines through the stone surrounds of the window and lights up the naked bodies entwined on the bed. As farmers plough their fields, politicians debate in Kirkwall, mothers bake oatcakes and draw up policies, and seals gather in the Bay of Skaill, two creatures lie entwined in bliss, oblivious to the world around, deep within their dreamspace. They float above the waters, dive into the deeps, surge through the waves and fly into the night sky, their wings emblazoned with water. They enter volcanoes, shafts of fire, waves of water, and emerge unscathed, bathed in light, floating on air. They are two creatures melted into one, in tune with themselves and in tune with nature. In this state of grace, they are invincible, alive, fired with erotic energy, surging with sensual desire, body, mind and soul in perfect harmony. They could emerge from this state to compose a symphony or catch fish with their fins. They could talk to their ancestors, cause peace to fall upon the earth like gold dust from the heavens. In this state of grace, they can do anything. The choice is theirs.

Sasha wakes first, rubbing her eyes, wondering where she is. Her limbs are entwined around Cowrie as if they are one breathing creature. She stays in this position, wondering if she dreamed this vision or if it really happened. Her body feels alive, energised, floating on air, yet sensual and soft. She remembers flying through the air, entering into volcanoes, diving to the ocean depths, being capable of anything her heart desires. Elation fills her, staying with her, as she recalls her mother talking about the dreamspace, that it was rare to reach this, but

169

it could empower a person to live their dreams. Her eyes float down Cowrie's body. She looks like an angel, her wings rapt around Sasha, her eyes still closed, her soft, rounded body flying out of a Botticelli painting, only a darker copper colour. She runs her fingers softly down Cowrie's cheeks, waking her gently, making her murmur. 'Sweet Sash, fin me forever.' She then moves softly back into sleep.

Sasha lies there another half-hour until Cowrie wakes. They gently untangle their bodies and prepare a bath together, running water heated from the peat fire into the old clawed bath. They share their memories of the experience and Sasha is blown away to find Cowrie also felt the same surges, the same awakening, also entered into dreamspace. It has inspired each of them similarly. They each rub the back of the other, marvelling at this shared magic, Cowrie recalling its beginnings with Peta on Great Turtle Island. Sasha is careful coming to the part of Cowrie's back which held the pain. But she need not be. It has gone, disappeared, now lies deep in the pit of the volcano, burned to the core, releasing her back into pain-free health. Sasha rubs harder, to make sure the wound has gone. Cowrie does not wince, but bubbles over with ideas for their shared storytelling session, not even noticing the fingers pressing her shell.

In the kitchen, Monique is rattling pots and shuffling papers. Exquisite smells start exuding from the old coal range, and soon the voices of DK and Uretsete are heard as they enter the house. Cowrie and Sasha dry each other, still elated, still soaring, and prepare to join them.

'Wow! You look amazing,' utters DK, as they emerge from the bathroom. 'I bet I know what you have been up to.'

Sasha winks and says, 'You'd never guess, DK, not in a million years.'

DK grimaces. 'Obvious, sister. You can't hide nuttin from me.' She winks at Uretsete, who pretends not to notice.

'We've been dreaming up a whale of a workshop,' says Cowrie, noticing the mound of tomatoes, red peppers, mustard greens and chives next to a steaming cheesy omelette, the smells wafting into her nostrils. 'We'll tell you our plans over this feast.'

The five of them tuck into Monique's delicious brunch, savouring the taste of fresh free-range farm eggs and local Orkney cheeses. The Birsay tomatoes taste like none they have eaten before and they are amazed such delicious vegetables could grow on an island with this climate. It feeds their desire to work up a garden for Morrigan, as a koha for their stay, filled with herbs and vegetables to go with her beloved tatties and turnips. They move onto plans for the storytelling workshops with Sasha and Cowrie on a high, filling them with sensuous suggestions, each one a symphony of pleasure for the mind to play with, full of the possibilities enriched by their stay on these magic islands of light, where semi-darkness invades the land for only a few hours before letting in the light again. There is little chance for the darkness to take hold over the summer months, but winter, as Morrigan warned them, is another reality.

[36]

'Don't yee know aboot the hoose on Sule Skerry?' asks the woman in the knitted dress with seals and otters embroidered into the design. Some of the workshop participants, mostly the older ones, nod their heads, but most of the younger ones look blank.

'Weel, oil tell thee then. Once upon a windy Skaill night, two fishers from the North Dyke area of Sandwick unhooked their dory from the noust in the Bay of Skaill and went oot fishin. The wind howled at them all night and whipped their boot way oot to sea. They thought they were doomed and the mists set in, then by dawn, they saw land rising from the fog. T'was the peedie island of Sule Skerry stuck out in the Atlantic off the coast of Orkney. They landed their boot and were taken aback to find a wee stoon cottage on the skerry. They knocked on the door and it opened and lo and behold theer stood the young Rowland lassie, who'd been amissing for quite some time.'

'I know them folks,' utters one of the children, delighted to recognise a name.

'Sure enough lassie, they still survive. Anyway, let me back to the story. She asked them in and they offered news aboot her kith and kin. She was happy to hear it n'all. Then they inquired as to how she arrived on the Sule Skerry. She said she'd been walking the shore at Leygabroo in the Bay of Skaill. She was after limpets and the like for bait. Her father had warned her never to turn her back to the waves. She forgot, and the moment she bent down, wet fins wrapped themselves aboot her peedie body an she was swept into the sea. The seal had taken her for his wife.'

'How could a seal do that?' asks young Ginger, his hair as aflame as his eyes. 'Easy, laddie, easy. For this seal was a selkie and could walk on land as well as the sea. He wanted a bride from the land to live with him in the sea.'

'So did she goo with him?'

'The wee lassie had no choice. But she soon adjusted and true it be he was a good selkie, better than many a man she'd find on land. Aye, that's for sure.' The woman licks her lips and continues. '"Anyway," she says, "I now live with this sealman and I like it, so tell my family I am safe." At this moment, a large seal flopped through the door from the sea, wetting the stone floor and making his way to the end of the hoose. Minutes later, a tall man appeared.'

'Was he the sealman?'

'Aye, lassie, he was indeed. He bade them good will and was in good cheer that their boot had made it through the storm. T'was weather to make yer glad to be a seal, he added, with a grin at the men. They chuckled nervously. Nevertheless, they ate the best fish that night, caught by the selkie, no less, and he laughed and told them he'd snatched the fish from the men's own hoose at Unigarth. They were amazed.'

'Couldn't they catch fish too?', asks a peedie lad.

'Aye, laddie, but not like the haddock this night. T'was the best fish they'd ever eaten, fresh and wriggling on the plate. Anyway, they bedded down for the night and woke to a glorious new dawn, and set sail to return to Sandwick to tell all the good folks at North Dyke aboot their adventures and the fate of the wee local lassie. Never a year had passed that this story was not told to their family and the sons and daughters since. So yee'll never see the peedie folk turning their backs to the waves at the Bay of Skaill, now will yee?' The woman sighs, picks up the hem of her knitted dress, making the seals and otters swim about the swirling seas of yarn and returns to her grassy seat at the workshop.

She is swamped by questions from younger and older folk and she answers them with immense patience, explaining all about the selkies and their lives and how we must keep telling these stories and make them live, because they are, she says, 'the lifeblood and soul of Orkney. Yee cannot have a life withoot stories. They are as much Orkney as oatcakes and peat-smoked salmon and Skara Brae.'

Camilla announces lunch and the group breaks to bring their offerings to the large trestle table laid out in the open field near the Ring of Brodgar. Baked tatties with melted cheese, oatcakes, date scones, smoked haddock and mackerel, cheeses ranging from light yellow to burnt orange, a huge pot of steaming clapshot heated over a fire, stuffed tomatoes and a range of sandwiches alight on the table, alongside salads of spinach and lettuce and tomato. One woman has brought along a Scots hare soup called Bawd Bree, and another, a pile of corn cobs from the hothouse, which they bake in their skins over the fire then peel to eat. The result is a wonderful feast which all the storytellers have contributed to. They lie about the green grass, spiked with wildflowers, dwarfed by the ancient stones nearby, and discuss the morning sessions while they eat.

Cowrie, Sasha, DK, Monique and Camilla meet for a brief moment to check all the workshops are running as planned. They are blown away by the richness of the tales told and the knowledge of their heritage that these Orcadians possess. Seldom have they held sessions where a large portion of people know stories about their own people and land, unless this is among indigenous groups who have kept this knowledge intact through extended family structures, where they have not been broken up and families split apart for survival. After assessing that all is going to plan, they return to their groups for the lunch and afternoon sessions.

Cowrie noticed that young Shelley from the seafood farm in Finstown was present at the morning session and had looked distinctively uncomfortable when Lallie Isbister had told her story about the seals of Skaill. A few of the other ones had nudged each other and nodded toward her, as if she too could be a modern version of the missing Skaill lassie who was taken away by the seals. She approaches Shelley, offering her some smoked haddock. Shelley refuses, saying she has eaten so much fish in her time that she has turned vegetarian. Cowrie holds back a sudden desire to tell her she could be a turtle and not a seal if she wished, since they mostly survive on seaweed and other vegetarian delights. Then she realises she too is playing into the selkie myths which have dogged Shelley for most of her teenage years, and pulls back. She then tempts her with some delicious salad, which Shelley takes onto her plate.

'How about some olives?' Cowrie asks.

Shelley looks askance. 'Too much like Neptune's necklace,' she says, screwing up her face at the thought of eating anything as salty and so much like the seaweed that drapes itself about the shores of Orkney.

'You always been in a fishing family then?' asks Cowrie, knowing full well she has.

'Aye. My dad was a fisher and my mum was a fisher's wife. That means you cook the fish and serve it up to family and guests and have long nights alone while your husband is out at sea.'

175

'Sounds like it can be a lonely life,' says Cowrie, thinking of Morrigan and her pattern of living, how hard it might be to work around this for anyone wanting a regular existence.

'Aye, it is. Especially if your dad loves his fishing more than his family, and other fishers more than his wife.' Shelley glances down at her shoes and winces. 'I shouldn't've said that. Kelpie was a good man indeed. He never meant no harm.'

'Kelpie. That name rings a bell,' says Cowrie, immediately interested. Wasn't this the name of Morrigan's lover, whose name was on the message inside the bag of peats? She listens intently.

'Aye, it's a common enough name. It was also the name of his boot. He died in that boot. It still sits inside me mother's back yard. She died a year later, from a broken heart.' Shelley picks at her food, more interested in getting her story off her chest.

'So where did you live after that?' asks Cowrie.

'Me mother's family. They never thought Kelpie was a good influence on me or mother. So they took me in to bring me up right. I still live at the back of their cottage but one day I want to escape to Scotland. I want to play the fiddle at the Edinburgh Fringe Festival. I once knew a boy who went there. He said it was a different world.'

'It is. We've just come from performing there, actually. I know a fiddle player who has a band of fiddlers. Maybe I could arrange for you to visit him. He'd also be interested in playing at the Orkney Folk Festival — so you'd have a bit in common.' Cowrie bites into a tomato from her plate.

Shelley pricks up her ears. 'I'd love that.' She looks over toward the ring and notices a lone figure staring out over the Loch of Harray and panics. She turns to Cowrie.

'Can we talk aboot it after the session today? I have to meet someone.' Cowrie agrees and watches as she walks back across the fields towards the Ring of Brodgar.

After a luscious feast, full to the brim, they begin the afternoon sessions, where they have to invent new stories based on their knowledge of the old folklore and the myths they have heard. The groups are abuzz with ideas and the land beneath them vibrates with their energy. Cowrie looks over toward the Ring, wondering how many stories the standing stones bear witness to after all these years. As the sun moves around, the shadows lengthen and the ring looks like a giant sundial in the distance. There will be a break for dinner and then the night performances will begin, culminating in a celebration around the ring at sunset, at about nine-thirty. Cowrie looks forward to this time, as she has not seen the impressive stone circle lit up by the setting sun lowering over the Loch of Stenness.

[37]

Morrigan looks up at the clock. It's a half-hour since Shelley said she'd be here — maybe. Looks like she's changed her mind. She edges off her seat at the inn and wanders over to Seafayre. A dory is tied to the dock unloading a haul of scallops. Damned fine ones too. She wouldn't mind knowing where they dredge. She leans against the door and watches as the women launch themselves into the large salty ponds, bringing out nets full of Orkney oysters, scallops, cockles, mussels and spoots still spitting into the air. She recalls Shelley throwing her the spoot, knowing it'd piss into her face. Still, the kid has had a hard time all these years. Time she knew the truth.

Moira from Cockle Farm looks up from her netting. 'Hullo there, Morrigan. You in for some spoots, then?' Clearly Shelley has told her the story. Moira grins.

'Not today, thanks, Moira. I'm after Shelley, actually. Know where she is?'

'Och, aye, lassie. She's up at the Ring with half the township spilling stories aboot the past n' fairies n' trows n' the like with those ferryloopers you brought back with yee from Edinburgh.'

'They're not into looping the ferry, Moira. They are here to find oot more about Orkney myths and legends and to run storytelling workshops for the local community education.' Morrigan puffs on her pipe for good measure.

'And a good deal more, some say,' adds Moira, with a chuckle.

Morrigan hates gossip and is annoyed by her

response. 'And what, pray Moira, else do yee think they're doing here?'

Moira is put on the spot and tries to wriggle out of it by concentrating hard on a spoot that has shot over the other side of the pool and is fast burrowing itself under a pile of cockles. Morrigan waits, silently, puffing on her pipe, until Moira can bear the silence no longer.

'Weel, some say, and I'm never one to agree with local tittle-tattle.' She takes a deep breath for this is always how she prefaces gossip. 'Some say that they are the likes that prefer women, you know. Not that there's nowt wrong with that, but they have strange ways, you know.'

'What kind of ways, Moira?' asks Morrigan, her eyebrows raised expectantly.

'Well, just queer, strange.' Moira looks around to make sure she is out of the hearing of others. 'They like to diddle-daddle with each other instead of how God made us — to be with men and to bear children.'

Morrigan draws in a breath, puffing out smoke rings as she concentrates on how she will word her next sentence. 'I think you might be wrong, there, Moira. Monique has had a child and so has Camilla. I don't know aboot the rest, but they all look like good child-bearing women if you ask me. Seems that you can choose to be with men or women and have children or not in a democratic society, I'd've thought.'

'It's against God's way, and you know it Morrigan. And so is communing with them seals. The devil's gotta make a person prefer an animal over his own kith and kin, or a woman instead of a man. That's God's law.'

'As interpreted by you, Moira. But when half the women on this island are in relationships with men that drink too much and then go home and bash up their wives, then yer can hardly say that's God's will, then, can yee?'

179

Moira grimaces, searching for another angle. 'And that's not all, Morrigan. Some say, not that I'm one of 'em, but I'm tellin' yee this for yer own good.' She bends over and whispers in Morrigan's ear. 'Some say, they are the witches of Skara Brae, returnin' to finish their business.' Moira coughs, as if it has been hard work bringing up this piece of gossip from the depths of her throat.

Morrigan looks at her then throws back her head and laughs loudly. 'And who, pray, are the witches of Skara Brae?'

Moira knits her brow, getting very serious, and hisses, 'You know very well. Them women that's locked up inside the walls of those old stone cottages. Ever since they uncovered the sand dunes and discovered them, there's been trouble. Men lost at sea, women dying in childbirth, crops being ruined and the like. They should cover up that damned Stone-age ruin and let it be. S'not right to dig up the dead, expose them to modern ways. It's God's will the storm covered the village and it's man's will to dig it up again and expose us to the ways of the devil.'

Morrigan takes a puff on her pipe, leans over to Moira and blows it in her face. 'Then that proves men are not always right, aye, Moira? There were men lost at sea and women dying in childbirth and crops failing long before they opened up Skara Brae.' She pauses a moment. 'Maybe, not that I think this Moira,' says Morrigan, prefacing her suggestion as Moira does her gossip, 'maybe you don't like Skara Brae because it makes a lot of money for Historic Scotland when your own croft struggled to survive. Maybe you should've prayed to the women of Skara Brae instead of cursing them, and maybe your wishes would have been heard.' Morrigan smiles, knowing this will irritate her.

'Tosh. Gobble-dee-gook. Yee carn't pray to the devil!' admonishes Moira, poking her net into a crevice in the pond, wanting to slam it down over Morrigan's head and silence her forever.

'And maybe, just maybe, not that I would think this, Moira, but yee know how the talk about Finstown fishers goes, p'raps yee're afraid of these women at Skara Brae and the ones I brought back, because they are different, they have cracked the code of male behaviour and invented lives for themselves outside of this system? It dinna mean they dislike men, just the systems of power. They are two different things.'

'One and the same to me,' spits out Moira. 'The women at Skara Brae lived separate from the men. It's not natural. They probably communed with the seals, like you, and for all I know yee could be one of 'em, bringin' these queer folks out here, setting them loose on the unsuspecting locals. If it weren't for yer affair with that Kelpie, I'd pick yer for one of 'em any day, dressing like a man all the time, takin' up fishin' for a lifestyle, drinkin' like the men. It ain't right.' Moira has spat it out now. She'd been holding this in for years. She turns her back on Morrigan and disappears into the packing room.

Morrigan leans against the door, looking out to sea, puffing smoke rings into the salty breeze. So that's what's eating her then. Kelpie's wife was her sister, and she knows they blamed her for the disappearance of Kelpie then his wife, and the abandonment felt by Shelley afterwards. But she never knew what Morrigan and Kelpie shared. It was much more than lust or sex or an affair. It was a meeting of souls, where their erotic desire led to a kind of spiritual fulfilment, enough that they could willingly complete the transformation to selkie and back again. They shared an undersea world together, one free from the constraints and rules of modern life, one where they focused on spirit rather than matter. They'd discovered hidden sides to their natures and felt the explosion of boundaries between human and animal, between the manmade and natural world. In the ocean, they were one and the same, on a new plane of existence, where communication between all beings is possible.

When Kelpie drowned, she joined him, but she had to return to an earthly existence by day and could only meet him by night. Once the selkies decided to take his wife, put her out of her grief, Morrigan seldom entered their world again and had to commune with Kelpie in spirit. She swam with him on isolated nights, when the moon was full and she could return to the Bay of Skaill by morning. But when Kelpie was caught in the net and left for dead, she had to try to save him. She'd hoped he could make it back to human form but he was too weak by then, could not even shed his skin. His last mumbled wish was that Morrigan tell Shelley he was finally dead and that her Bonnie was happily with another selkie, and who her true mother was. He wanted Shelley to live her life to the full. He'd made Morrigan promise she would look after Shelley, and she made that pact. Then she buried him. But now, she has to get Shelley's trust, which looks hard when Shelley does not even want to meet her.

The wind blows the smell of seaweed into Morrigan's face as she walks along the rocks. She cannot give up. She must keep trying, for Kelpie's sake. There's nothing else she can do. She returns to her van and heads out to the Ring of Brodgar. Maybe she can find Shelley and talk to her in private. Maybe she'd be more relaxed at the ring and surrounded by the storytellers. Maybe the standing stones would give their energy, make it easier to bridge the huge gulfs between them, let Shelley understand the depth of their relationship, and that she was the result of their first lovemaking, that Morrigan is her birth mother.

Moira watches the van from the tiny windows in the packing room until it disappears around the corner. Bad blood, that Morrigan. She's an evil one. Looks like a man, dresses like a man. Sings to the seals. It's not natural. She's bound to be a witch, or a dyke, or both. Her father was the same. Had a bit of the trow in him, that one. Mind you, Bonnie was hardly the perfect wife, neither. Had an affair with the milkman and regretted it after Kelpie disappeared. The guilt sent her a bit looney. Little wonder the seals took her then. Still, at least she'll be back with Kelpie now, though God's witness, I'd die if I had to live amongst all that wet tangle and slithery monsters. She pushes the last oysters into the package and seals it with her left hand while taking a fag out of her pocket with her right hand. Time for a break, she reckons. She's deserved it today.

[38]

Shelley saw Morrigan entering the stone circle while she was talking to Cowrie and suddenly remembered she was supposed to be at the inn. She quickly arranged to meet Cowrie later. She wants to avoid any confrontation or Morrigan spilling selkie stories in public up here. It's fine to tell selkie myths, but once the boundaries collapse and your entire family is taken by the seals, then it is another reality entirely. She quickens her pace so as to reach Morrigan before she gets it into her head to join the crowd. Morrigan is so unpredictable, you never quite know what she may get up to next.

Cowrie watches from a distance as Shelley meets her friend. A very tall lad by the look of his shape. He stands with his back to the women, looking out over the Loch of Harray, where small brightly coloured dinghies lie waiting on the sands, their sterns lapping in the loch. Maybe Shelley has a boyfriend? Someone she can share intimacies with. She needs that. Shelley reaches the figure and they stand at some distance from each other. Maybe they have had a rift over something? Cowrie turns her back on them and begins helping to clear the dishes and prepare for the afternoon session.

'I'm Sully Bancroft and ee'd leek to tell you aboot the Finfolk and how the beggar saved the ole' Mill o' Skaill,' says a man with long hair and a grey beard. 'Once there was a mill at Bay o' Skaill where folk came to have their corn ground. But the Finfolk who lived in the bay also liked the corn meal and so they'd swim in at night, scare the miller till he was half-dead with fright, and carry off the meal into the deep blue sea. This went on for many a moon, till the miller had to close down his mill.'

'How could the Finfolk carry the meal inta' the sea, cos it woold get all wet,' asks a peedie lad from Sandwick.

'Aye, laddie, there's no telling how the Finfolk like their meal. Happens they might like it all wet, being folk from the sea. Now, where was I then? Aye, the miller gave up the ghost and everyone else was too frightened to take over the mill. The stories had spread aboot the island like fire in the heather. Until one day this beggar comes along and says she knows how to get rid of the Finfolk. She asks them for a pot, a peat fire, some salt-water, kail and a ladle. Some folk scorned her requests, but then again, they was right keen to get rid of the Finny Ones. So she lay in wait with her goodies until the Finned Ones, seeing a fire at the mill, swam in and finned their way up the bay to see what was cookin'. When they got close enough, she ladled out the kail and boiling water from the pot on the peat fire and threw it all over them. They screamed and ran aboot, flames flaring oota their fins, then dived inta the sea and never returned to t' Mill o' Skaill.'

'Did they die of burns?' asks a wee girl, concerned.

The old man looks at her, seeing the pain in her eyes. 'No, lassie, for they made it back to the water in time. They had scarred fins, but could still swim, na doot.'

The wee lassie breathes a sigh of relief and he gets back to his tale. 'After that, the miller returned and started grinding corn again. A caisie was hung ootside the door for Skaill folks to put their meal into so the beggar would never be hungry again. You'd see her doon on the beach, gathering stoons, making a driftwood fire, and eating the cornmeal to her heart's desire. And the Finned Ones never bothered the millar again.'

'So wer'd they go, the Fins?'

'Back oot to sea, to find another place to live. They're very resourceful, them Finfolk. So if you ever see one, never under-estimate them,' he adds, with a note of caution.

The audience are keen on hearing more about the Finfolk, and a woman from Quoyloo, Bessie, knows more. 'My mother and hers and hers before told me aboot how the Finfolk lost the sacred 'n holy island of Eynhallow. Let me tell it to thee now.' She settles her rolls of flesh around her like a skirt, comfortably full of clapshot and oatcakes, and continues her tale. It is a long story, full of mystery, as she tells them about the man of Thorodale, whose wife was pulled into the sea by the Finfolk, and how, in retaliation, he got his sons to help get revenge. 'One orange dawn, he saw an island rise from the sea, the holy land of Eynhallow, and he bid his sons row with him, each carrying a caisie of salt. Their boot was surrounded by huge whales, the like of which had not been seen in a while, and they knew they'd been sent by the Finfolk to take them off their path. One whale opened his huge jaws and it looked like the whole boot, men an' all, would be swallowed by the giant. So the man threw some salt into the whale's throat and he splashed aboot in pain then sank back into the sea. Next they were distracted by some mermaids sent by the Finfolks, so he cast out crosses made from dried tangles and they screamed in fear of God and drowned themselves in the sea.

Finally, they arrived at the island and a huge monster with trunks appeared. They threw salt in his eyes and he screamed and rolled away. Then a Finman appeared and challenged them. They threw him a cross made from a sticky grass called cloggirs. Now the Finfolk are heathens and they dinna like crosses, so it stuck to his forehead and he screeched with agony. For this was the Fin who'd dragged Thorodale's wife into the sea. Then the man and his sons went aboot the island throwing salt at Finfolk and their wives and their animals and all of them screamed and fled for the sea. They began their task of making nine salt rings around the island, but the last was never finished, making Eynhallow still a holy island. Now, if you try to tether an animal, it's said the iron stake will jump oot of the earth. If you cut corn after the moon has risen, the stalks will ooze blood onto the hallowed ground. So the Finfolk lost the island of Eynhallow. T'was the last island to be made sacred, that's for sure.' She stretches her arms and looks into the large eyes of the children.

There is a long silence, and one of them asks a disarming question. 'Why was folks so horrid to the Finpeople? Seems like they just wanted love.'

Bessie looks at the young girl whose eyes are sea-green and full of hope. 'Aye, yee might be right there. But then they was considered heathens. They didn't follow the ways of God and people was scared of anything different in those days.'

'Has it changed now? Are they still scared of Finfolk?'

This one takes Bessie by surprise. She pauses a moment. 'Like as not, some folk are always frightened by those who are different, who dare to stand oot among the crowd.' She thinks of her own son, himself a gay lad, long married to a beautiful dark island man, and how hard she'd worked to accept them, how she'd used God as an excuse for her fear of difference as well. 'Aye, it takes time for acceptance. Maybe that's why these stories abound. They are aboot trows an' fairies and selkies and Finfolk and people's fear of them. Maybe they are just projections of our own fears too.'

187

Bessie surprises herself. She'd never consciously thought of this before, and neither had Cowrie, who nods her head in agreement. She's distracted a little, since Shelley has not returned to the group. She'd not noticed her going but now neither she nor the man are at the ring or anywhere to be seen. Cowrie hopes she'll return for the celebrations around the ring tonight, so she can pass on her Edinburgh contact and make sure it is followed through before she leaves the island.

She cannot imagine leaving now. She has become very fond of the endless light, the ancient stories lying under the earth, waiting to be unfolded by the next generation, the powerful tradition of myth and storytelling that has sustained these island people through the worst of blustery northern winters, where the dark takes over and there's only a few hours of sunlight a day. And the people themselves, tough, gentle, strong, complex, God-fearing and politically liberal all at once. These are islands of contrasts, colonised by so many different cultures, and yet embracing them all. They are islands of extremes, in climate, nature, mood and manner.

And most of the extremes are embodied in Morrigan, that attractive, annoying, charming, moody pirate of the seas. Morrigan would fit in well with the Finfolk and they'd've taken to her. They both challenge authority and do it devilishly, with a twinkle in the eye. She imagines Morrigan swimming up to the mill at the Bay of Skaill, attracted to the light of the fire, keen to taste the cornmeal, even at the expense of the miller and smiles at the thought.

[39]

Fiona floats on the surface as the sun sets above her, unconcerned about the squid passing her by. She has made a pact not to eat squid after one of them unwittingly helped her to distract the shark away from Sandy. It's more difficult for Sandy, whose mouth waters as he watches such fat squid thrusting their way forward, full of tasty morsels and just what he needs tonight. He bites his lip and instead chases after a haughty haddock who thinks nothing of flicking his tail right in Sandy's face.

In the distance, they hear the purr of a motor and recognise its tone. Soon a blue-bottomed dory circles the area and Sandy pokes his nose, full of fresh haddock, into the air to let her know they are there, then dives down to join Fiona, now at the ocean floor, to cleanse his palate with seaweed. Above, the dory idles a while then drops anchor. It lands in the kelp near to them and disturbs a school of mackerel feeding below. Sandy scoops one up in his mouth and downs it before Fiona has time to scold him for his greed.

A clanking from above and then a pair of giant fins break the surface of the water, surrounded by bubbles. Once they disappear, a seal emerges, and dives down to greet them. The seal circles around to make sure she has the right couple. She'd not noticed the gash in one fin until now.

'Sandy, Fiona. I'm right glad to see you both agin. It's bin a long time.'

'Aye, Morrigan. We'd wondered what'd kept yee from coming. We thought maybe ye'd stay above ground from now on, never to return.'

189

'This'll be my last swim. I've news for you both. Kelpie got caught in a net and died oot of the sea before he had a chance to shed his skin. It was a long and painful letting go, but he's laid to rest on my farm and so's the past, at long last.'

'Does Shelley know all this yet?', asks Fiona, concerned.

'She does indeed. She found it hard to take but I convinced her it was true. I took her oot to the grave and showed her the ring Kelpie gave me and told her the whole story. She wept and wept.' Morrigan fins the water to keep afloat, a bit out of practice.

'It's a good thing yee've done, Morrigan. She had to know sometime. Poor love, she always looked lost, even when her folks was alive.' Fiona nibbles at the edge of the dabberlocks, unable to stop herself munching her favourite food.

'Aye, it's a right good thing for yee, Morrigan. Lay it all to rest. The past is best left in the past and yee can never return to what was, no matter how hard yee try.' Sandy thinks about his former life as he says this, referring to he and Fiona as well.

Morrigan looks relieved, as if a huge weight has left her. She nods toward Sandy's fin. 'An how did yee get that gash, old fella?' Sandy eagerly tells her about the close escape from a great white shark and Morrigan enjoys the story immensely. The seahorses swing from their seaweed branches, dangling in the tide as if they are listening to the story too, and a flatfish rolls his eyes from the ocean floor, hoping he will not be their meal tonight. Sandy holds out his fin for Morrigan to see the gash where he ripped it on the rocks while escaping. Morrigan thinks how like the old Sandy this is. He carries his wounds as if in battle, be that from a hoe or a scythe or a shark. She chuckles to herself.

Once Sandy has finished his tale and Fiona has added the part about her time in the crevice, she asks Morrigan if Shelley knows the truth about who is really her mother. Morrigan flinches, twists her tail in discomfort. She'd never realised that Fiona, or anyone else knew about this.

'How did you guess?' she asks. 'Did Kelpie tell you?'

'Aye,' replies Sandy, cleaning his whiskers with his fin. 'Kelpie was right proud of young Shelley and he told us you was the true mother of the bairn. We never told Bonnie, of course. Evidently, she always thought Shelley was his niece, abandoned by her own mother who flew the nest for Australia and just a baby when they met. She took her on as her own and reckoned it was better that Shelley thought that too. Bonnie might've treated her rough if she knew you were the true mother. It was best left that way for all, Kelpie said. Bonnie swam away to live in Shetland with her new selkie lover, and there she stays as far as I know. She is a happier lass in the sea than ever she was on land, so I'm right pleased aboot that.'

'Me too,' replies Morrigan. 'It's a relief. I was always concerned aboot her though nobody would have known.'

'You hide yer feelings a lot, Morrigan. You could do with more lessons below sea,' adds Fiona. 'Time you made some changes now Kelpie is gone. You need to make a new start.'

'Think I will,' replies Morrigan, her eyes following a beautiful haddock as he proudly swishes by.

'Keep yer flashers off that fella,' warns Sandy. 'He's a right bugger.' They laugh and swim deeper into the kelp.

For some time, they catch up on news and then the moment comes for Morrigan to say her farewells and surface for the last time. They are sad to see her go, despite her gruffness when ruffled. They watch from the deep as Morrigan fins her way to the surface and emerges amidst a show of bright lights dazzling in the sky, a rainbow of colours and sparkling stars shooting through the heavens. Morrigan leaps over the side of the dory for the final time, sad to be leaving the sea, glad to be starting again. This time, she will try to be more consistent, not just swing with her moods.

Above her, a star shoots from the sky and splashes into the sea, followed by a fiery constellation resembling the northern lights. A harbinger of hope.

[40]

'Congratulations, Camilla, you did an excellent job organising this venue.' Monique pats her on the shoulder. Camilla is not so bad after all. Bit of a control freak but definitely organised when it comes to producing the goodies. Around them, the storytellers are preparing for their final performances, dressing up for the occasion in the clothes of their characters, and fires have been started around the farmer's land, lighting up the Ring of Brodgar.

'The best is yet to come. You wait,' adds Camilla, just a speckle of a twinkle in her eye.

'You mean the performances?' asks Monique.

'You could say that, with a bit of help from Heaven,' replies Camilla.

I wish she'd leave heaven out of the equation, thinks Monique. Her fundamentalist background always has to surface somewhere. But tonight is not a night for differences, rather to celebrate our common strengths. Monique changes the subject. 'Did Morrigan ever tell you why she called herself Ellen in Scotland?'

'Turns out it is her first name and she uses it rarely, mostly outside of Orkney. She reckons she is a different creature once she leaves the islands.'

'She sure is,' replies Monique, grinning. They both return to help their groups prepare for the celebration.

Cowrie notices that Shelley has returned to the circle and looks a bit pale. She takes her aside and asks if everything is okay. Shelley spills out everything, to a stunned Cowrie, and at the end all she can do is hug her closely. 'Well, I reckon you can celebrate a bloody fine mother, even if she's unconventional, and even if she's not the one who physically raised you.'

Shelley is about to grimace, when she thinks about the stories over their day together, and how Bessie filled her in on the afternoon session, telling her how the children asked such amazing questions and how she had a chance to surprise herself by her answers. Shelley is determined to try to get along with Morrigan, even if it takes some time. Just because she is different doesn't mean she is no good, thinks Shelley. At least she is alive and there for me. She tells Cowrie about her discussion with Bessie and asks what she thinks. Cowrie encourages her to try to get along with Morrigan and suggests she ask Morrigan to take her to the next fringe festival once she has made contact with the fiddlers. Maybe she could stay with them in Edinburgh for a while if Morrigan agrees. Cowrie promises she will broach the topic with Morrigan and Shelley kisses her on the cheek in thanks.

By now the twenty-seven standing stones in the magic ring are surrounded by fairies and Finfolk, selkies and trows. 'Never a scene like this was witnessed since the women of Skara Brae stood around these stoons themselves,' laughs Bessie, rejoicing in the atmosphere of joy and celebration. Men and women and children, young and old, some descended from selkies, some from Finfolk, some from Norsemen and others from the Scots and Irish and Celts and Picts, hold hands and dance around the Ring of Brodgar as the sun sets over the Loch of Stenness. Between stories, they sing and play the flute and fiddle.

Sasha recounts the story her Canadian Inuit grand-mother told her about the origin of the Sea Spirit and how the fingers cut from the girl by her father as she tried to get back into their boat caused seals to come to life in the sea. Then she tells the Netsilik Eskimo version where Nuliajuk's finger stumps spring to life in the sea and rise to the surface crying like seals, and how Nuliajuk became the mother of all sea creatures, and a woman of great powers whom Inuit are taught to respect. She enacts the stories as she did at the festival and the Orcadians are moved. Bessie responds by telling of the giant stoorworm who could only be subdued by a young Orcadian sailing into his stomach with a burning peat which he lodged into its liver. The stoorworm screamed and its tongue lashed the skies nearly pulling down the moon, then crashed back into the sea, its forked tongue cutting off Denmark and Norway and creating the Baltic Sea. Still screaming, the stoorworm lurched its head from the waves and crashed down again, causing his teeth to splash out into the ocean, creating the islands of Orkney. And so the islands of Shetland and Faroe also sprang to life. Then the defeated giant lay dormant and became the body of Iceland, its fiery volcanoes testament to the Orcadian peat still burning in its liver. The crowd draws in its breath as Sasha enacts the story while Bessie relays it.

Cowrie thinks about the similarity in the Inuit tales of the creation of the seals from the fingers, the Orcadian story about the creation of these islands from the stoorworm's teeth and the Pacific version where the fins of floating turtles were cut off to form groups of islands. Maybe it is in ancient storytelling that our shared roots can be found, where a common thread for the future lies, and all the stories require some form of sacrifice to achieve change. She looks around the faces of the storytellers and musicians. Keri was right. They have become the heart and muscles and mind of something perilous and new, something strange and growing and great.

As the moon rises, a dazzling display of lights appears high in the sky and startles the storytellers, leaving them looking up in awe. Camilla smiles. She'd planned the entire event to coincide with the aurora borealis and kept it secret from them all. Monique now realises what she meant by the heavens giving a helping hand. She smiles, thinking this Camilla has more to her than meets the eye.

There's another creature believing this right now, as she lands ashore at Finstown and jumps into the van, heading for the ring. The aurora borealis is still showering her dazzling display on the storytellers, arms linked in awe, looking up to the night sky, when a van pulls up at the shores of the Loch of Harray. A figure emerges from the van and quietly walks over the fields and joins hands between Camilla and Shelley. Shelley looks to her left and smiles. Morrigan smiles back. This is at least a start.

The stones are lit by all the colours of the rainbow and glow with pride at witnessing a new awakening of ritual. Just like the old days. When the women of Skara Brae celebrated with their men folk under the starry skies, when each harvest brought a new celebration, each animal who gave its life was honoured, when people did not need to bear arms against each other, because the common good was deemed more important than individual needs. The moon smiles down on the Ring of Brodgar. The stones are witnessing the dawning of a new age.

Deep beneath the Bay of Skaill, two seals prepare to leave for warmer oceans, knowing their work is done here and they can return for the next season. From the walls of Skara Brae, the old women wail a farewell to protect them on their journey, then their spirits return to the Ring of Brodgar, as they always promised to do.

Cowrie notices two elderly women, set apart from the group. She is about to welcome them forward, when they disappear into the stones. Nobody else seems to see them. Maybe it's a trick of the light. She looks up into the night sky, dazzled by the starry circus. The colours light up the faces of the group. It is then that she notices Morrigan, one hand in Shelley's and the other in Camilla's. She smiles. Sasha holds her own hand, squeezes it gently.

Out beyond the breakers, two seals swim into the rainbow-splashed seas, their new journey started amidst a sky full of sizzling stars. But they know, like the women, they will return to these Orcadian waters, for they have experienced the blessing of the Finfolk and responded to the Song of the Selkies.

Select Bibliography

Books consulted during research for *Song of the Selkies*:

Chapel Preservation Committee. *Orkney's Italian Chapel*, printed by the Orcadian Ltd, Kirkwall, Orkney.

Lamb, Gregor. *Hid Kam Intae Words: Orkney's Living Language*, Byrgisey, Birsay, Orkney, 1986.

Lamb, Gregor. *Orkney Wordbook: A Dictionary of the Dialect of Orkney*, Byrgisey, Birsay, Orkney, 1988.

McAuley, John M. *Seal-Folk and Ocean Paddlers: Sliochd nan Ron*, The White Horse Press, Isle of Harris, Outer Hebrides, 1998.

Muir, Tom. *The Mermaid Bride and other Orkney Folk Tales*, The Kirkwall Press, Kirkwall, Orkney, 1998.

Ritchie, Anna. *Prehistoric Orkney*, (Historic Scotland Series), B.T. Battsford Ltd, London, 1995.

Ritchie, Anna. *The Brochs of Gurness and Midhowe*, (Historic Scotland Series), B.T. Battsford Ltd, London 1993.

Skara Brae, *Maes Howe*, Historic Scotland booklets.

Stewart, Bob & Matthews, John. *Legendary Britain*, Blandford Press, London, 1993.

Walsh, Mary. *Walks in Orkney*, Westmorland Gazette, Cumbria, 1994.

Glossary

Aotearoa	New Zealand
arohanui	much love
caisie	Orkney for basket, usually made of heather but sometimes of grass or reeds
ceilidh	dance within festival
ferryloopers	non-Orcadians who come and go on the ferry
Finfolk	the fin people of early Orkney myths
giro	UK term for unemployment benefits
gracefins	invented term for dolphins
hei matau	bone fishhook worn around the neck
jandals	thongs, slippers (US)
ka pae	that's good, that's fine
kai moana	seafood
karakia	prayer
karanga	chant
kelpie	originally a water monster in Orkney
ki'i pohaku	Hawai'ian petroglyphs or rock drawings
kia kaha	stay strong
Kina	sea egg
koauau	Maori bone flute played through the nose
kohanga reo	lit. language nest — Maori pre-school conducted entirely in Maori
kura kaupapa	Maori secondary school conducted entirely in Maori
longfins	whales
mahalo	thank you (Hawai'ian)
manuhiri	karanga
maranga mai	come together, gather round

nousts	moulds in the rocks where the prows of boats have been for many years worn into the rocks or sand or clay
Orkneyinga	book describing the history of Orkney and saga and book have their own historical centre in Orkney of the same name
pahoehoe	lava rocks (Hawai'i)
pakeha	white person (Maori)
peedie	little, wee (Orkney)
selkie	seal woman. Many ancient myths surround the selkies. Book explains context.
shaldro	pied oyster catcher or torea (from earlier Cowrie series). This bird has a symbolic role in the Cowrie series.
Siliyik	story-telling performance group. (Chumash Indian term for 'sacred enclosure in the dancing ground')
taniwha	mythical beast; water monster
tatties	potatoes
tototoko	Maori talking stick, sacred
trow	troll
waiata	song
whanau	family
youngfin	young finned creatures

Also by Cathie Dunsford

Cowrie
Cathie Dunsford
Cath Dunsford's first novel (of a series I hope) is a gentle determined, insightful and womanful book.

Keri Hulme

ISBN: 1-875559-28-2

The Journey Home: Te Haerenga Kainga
Cathie Dunsford
This is lesbian fantasy dripping with luscious erotic imagery.

NZ Herald

ISBN 1-875559-54-X

Manawa Toa: Heart Warrior
Cathie Dunsford
The novel is suffused with Maori culture, women's culture, and a passion for the beauty of Aotearoa, the land and the sea.

Sue Pierce, *Lesbian Review of Books*

ISBN: 1-875559-69-8

If you would like to know more about Spinifex Press write for a free catalogue or visit our website

Spinifex Press
PO Box 212 North Melbourne
Victoria 3051 Australia
<http://www.spinifexpress.com.au>